MW00930083

The Renegade Apprentice
An Heirs of Destiny Novel

By Andy Peloquin

Copyright. First Edition

Andy Peloquin

©2019, Andy Peloquin

ALL RIGHTS RESERVED. This book contains material protected under International and Federal Copyright Laws and Treaties. Any unauthorized reprint or use of this material is prohibited. No part of this book, including the cover and photos, may be reproduced or transmitted in any form or by any means, electronic or mechanical, including photocopying, recording, or by any information storage and retrieval system without express written permission from the author / publisher. All rights reserved.

Any resemblance to persons, places living or dead is purely coincidental. This is a work of fiction.

Table of Contents

Chapter One

"The two of you ought to be ashamed." Lectern Tinis' pudgy lips pursed in disapproval as his mud-colored eyes darted between the boys before him. "Your service to the Master is one of learning. You will one day be scholars, men of learning and refinement. Not the brutes and thugs I see before me."

Evren wiped the trickle of blood from his mouth. His knuckles ached, but Verald's jaw would ache far worse for far longer. That alone was worth a busted lip and a black eye.

"As Lecterns-in-training, you are to use words to settle your disputes, never your fists." Lectern Tinis folded his hands over his heavy gut and reclined in the over-stuffed armchair behind his ornate desk. "Those pendants you wear mark you as servants to the Master. Do I need to remind either of you what the words inscribed thereupon say?"

Evren resisted the urge to touch the platinum crescent moon that hung around his neck. He'd thumbed it so many times the words "Servitude, Humility, Concord" had faded.

The Lectern leaned forward, and the table creaked beneath his weight. "Have either of you ought to say for yourselves?"

Evren shot a glance at Verald, who sat stiffly in the hard-backed wooden chair beside him. Neither of the two young men spoke—Lectern Tinis' punishment would only worsen if they offered excuse or justification.

"So be it." Lectern Tinis gave a dramatic sigh and waved a fat hand toward the door. "To your cells, the both of you. Remain there until Lectern Uman comes for you."

Evren clenched his fists, but he couldn't stop the shudder from running down his spine. There was no worse punishment than this.

"I warn you," the Lectern said, leaning forward in his chair, "resist the urge to pursue whatever grievance exists between you. Our service to the Master consists not only of seeking his holy wisdom but aspiring to follow the example of virtue and nobility he has set for us. A day of abstinence from food and water should suffice to remind you of your duties to our god."

"Yes, Lectern Tinis," Evren and Verald intoned in unison. Together, they bowed to the Lectern then turned to leave.

As always, Evren was struck by the richness of the Lectern's rooms. Tapestries worked with gold and silver thread hung from the white marble walls, and the suite adjoining the priest's office held a massive four-poster canopied bed, a plush divan, and a shelf laden with rare volumes—no doubt "borrowed" from the Vault of Stars.

The halls outside Lectern Tinis' rooms were equally adorned with valuables: bronze vases, prized Fehlan ice candles sitting in brass candlesticks, teak furniture, and gold and silver statuettes worth a fortune. No outsiders ever visited this section of the temple, so none but the Lecterns knew the full extent of the wealth housed in the Master's Temple.

That wasn't the only truth known exclusively to the Lecterns. These halls concealed more dark, twisted secrets than the rest of Vothmot would ever know.

He and Verald walked through the lamp-lit corridors toward the staircase that descended five floors to ground level. The two apprentice Lecterns remained silent until they left the ornately decorated High Lectern's floor behind.

"You bastard!" Verald growled in a low whisper.

"Coward," Evren retorted without looking at the apprentice. "Picking on those weaker than you."

"You watch your back, fifth-year." Verald's voice was quiet but thick with menace. "The temple's got too many shadows. Never know what'll jump out at you when your back's turned."

Evren's fists balled, but before he could whirl on the boy, a pair of green-and-silver-robed Lecterns appeared in the stairway below them. The two apprentices bowed as they made way for the priests to pass, but the Lecterns paid them no heed. The youths were beneath their notice until they were accepted as full-fledged priests in service to Kiro, the Master. Only the handful of Lecterns—including Tinis and Uman— tasked with training the apprentices even spoke to them. Conversation had no place in a life spent in meditation, silent study, and chores.

"You know where to find me," Evren snarled when the Lecterns had disappeared around the bend in the staircase. "Don't think just because you're a sixth-year that won't stop me from giving you another beating."

Evren stepped close and stared into Verald's eyes. At thirteen, Verald was a year older than him and nearly a hand taller, but his rail-thin arms couldn't drive a punch with enough force to slow Evren down. He'd taken far worse knocks from the eighth-year apprentices.

"Verald!" A hard, angry voice echoed through the stairway.

Verald blanched and turned toward the speaker. "Dracat, I—"

"Shut up!" Dracat, a dark-haired ninth-year and captain of Grey Tower's fighters, stalked up the stairs toward them. "I hear you two got caught fighting?"

"I-It was nothing, Dracat," Verald stammered.

"Nothing?" Dracat loomed over Verald, his face a mask of rage. "Tinis is giving you the hunger treatment, right? Locked in your room for a day?"

"Yes, but—"

Dracat slapped him, hard, and the *crack* echoed off the dark stone walls of the hall. "No buts, Verald. I don't give a rat's arse if you're kept out of the matches, but I had four imperials riding on Evren here getting laid out cold in the third round." The older boy's eyes went to Evren. "All of Grey Tower's been looking forward to watching Engerack beat

7

the snot out of you. Too many of us lost on your bout with Warner to let that go by unpunished."

Evren gritted his teeth. Engerack was a seventh-year that weighed nearly as much as Lectern Tinis, but years spent mucking the stables had turned his body to hard muscle. He doubted he could have done more than stunned the larger seventh-year, and he'd resigned himself to a few weeks of painful recovery. Lectern Tinis' punishment almost came as a reprieve—until he remembered Lectern Uman would be paying him a visit. He'd take a year of Dracat's bare-knuckled fights any day.

"Don't think this gets you out of it," Dracat snapped, his teeth bared in a snarl. He bent low and whispered into Evren's ear. "I might just have to put you against Oldsek for this."

Evren's gut clenched. Even Engerack feared Oldsek—the wiry eighth-year hadn't lost a match since he bit Vorth's nose off.

"Let's go, Verald." Dracat seized the fifth-year by the collar and dragged him down the stairs, then shoved him down a side hallway that led to Grey Tower, one of the four minarets rising from the Master's Temple. "We'll be waiting for you," he called over his shoulder. "I just hope starvation and thirst doesn't weaken you too much."

Evren's heart hammered a panicked beat in his chest as he hurried down a hallway in the opposite direction. The distance to White Tower might have been a few hundred steps, but dread made it feel like a hundred leagues. Dracat could out-cruel anyone in White Tower. Evren's next fight, whenever it happened, would be heavily weighted against him. The best he could hope for was a beating without any broken bones.

The main area of the Master's Temple reeked of grandeur, with high-vaulted ceilings, plush Al Hani rugs, and more ornate woven tapestries of every conceivable hue. People came from all around Einan to see the Grand Chapel's breathtaking stained glass window, or to bask in the sunlight that streamed through the enormous glass dome in the central nave—the light of the Master's wisdom, some said, able to turn even a fool wise.

But there were many sections that the people of Vothmot never saw: the Grand Lectern's rooftop suite, the luxurious rooms of the High

Lecterns, and the vast knowledge stored deep underground in the Vault of Stars. And the dingy, freezing cells where the apprentice Lecterns spent their ten years of training to become priests in service to Kiro, the Master, father of the gods.

The main temple building served as home to the Lecterns, and the apprentices' cells filled the lowest levels of the temple's four minarets. Close to a hundred boys between the ages of eight and seventeen lived in Black, White, Grey, and Crystal Towers.

The corridors that led into White Tower were simple, all bare stone walls and floors, lacking the elegance of the main temple. He dreaded running into any of the other White Tower apprentices—Rhyris, the ninth-year who served as captain of White Tower's fighters, would lay into him for his scuffle with Verald. No doubt he had a lot of money riding on Evren's fight with Engerack—which side had he bet on?

Down one floor he went, then he turned into the stark hallway that led to the apprentices cells. He breathed a sigh of relief as he reached the plain wooden door to his cell. He'd made it without trouble.

The cell doors bore deadbolts and padlocks, but the Lecterns rarely used them. They had apprentices to keep even the most stubborn and problematic—those like Evren—in line.

The interior of his cell was dark, with no windows, candles, or lanterns to provide illumination. The thin strip of lamplight leaking through the barred slot on the cell's door was wasted on the featureless stone walls, floor, and ceiling of the cramped chamber. Four steps wide and five steps long; he'd paced it a thousand times during the many days he'd spent locked away as punishment for some misdeed.

The Lecterns believed apprentices needed nothing more than bare stone cells—nothing to distract them from their devotion to the Master. Only once they were accepted into the temple's service did they receive a proper room, and never any as nice as Lectern Tinis' luxurious chamber. By all appearances, his duties as caretaker for the apprentices in the Master's Temple afforded him more luxuries than the other Lecterns. Either that, or Lancred was right and Tinis was dipping into the temple's coffers to line his pockets.

"Evren?"

The quiet voice came from the pile of straw heaped against the room's eastern wall, the only thing resembling furniture in the bare chamber.

"It's me, Daver." Evren knelt beside the bed. "How's the head?"

"Better, I think." The mattress rustled as Daver tried to sit up.

Evren studied Daver's forehead in the dim lamplight. The blood leaking from the gash above his right eyebrow had begun to crust. Verald couldn't hit hard enough to give even a smaller, weaker fifth-year like Daver a concussion.

"Stay down, Daver." Evren pushed the boy's shoulders back down to the sparse bed. "You remember what happened that time I took a head hit against Lancred?"

Daver gave a little laugh. "You emptied your guts on Rhyris' new sandals."

"The dizziness'll pass with a bit of rest," Evren said, and he couldn't help smiling at the memory. Rhyris had beaten him soundly, but the leather sandals the ninth-year had been so proud of had never been seen again. Here in the Master's Temple, that was as close to happiness as it got.

"You shouldn't have intervened, Evren," Daver said in a quiet voice. "Verald's going to find a way to get even with you, and Dracat and Rhyris are going to be pissed that you missed your fight."

"I'm not worried about them. I'm just worried about you, Daver." Evren sat on the floor beside the head of the bed he and the smaller boy shared. "I told you I'd watch out for you, and so I will."

"But—"

"What's done is done," Evren cut in. "I've gone without food and water for longer than a day. I'll manage."

"I'll see if I can sneak something in for you," Daver said.

"No!" Evren's retort cracked like a whip. "The Lecterns will know if you do. They'll punish the both of us. Just let me get through it."

Daver drew in a breath, but before he could argue, Evren gripped his shoulders. "Swear it, Daver. Swear on the Master that you won't try to sneak anything in here."

Silence echoed in the cell for a moment. "I swear I won't sneak any food or drink in here," Daver said quietly.

The tension drained from Evren's shoulders, and he leaned his head against the cold stone wall. He'd never had a brother, never had much in the way of family. Daver was as close as it got, so he'd do whatever he could to keep the smaller, weaker apprentice out of harm's way. Even if that meant taking a beating or one of Lectern Uman's "lessons" in his place.

Ice flooded Evren's veins as he heard the unmistakable *slap, scrape* of Lectern Uman's footsteps in the hall beyond. A moment later, the door to his cell groaned open and the Lectern himself appeared in the opening. The lamplight in the hall outlined his twisted, shortened right leg, his thick shoulders, and high forehead.

"Evren, my boy," Lectern Uman said in the same rich, solemn voice that read out the afternoon service in the Grand Chapel. "Lectern Tinis tells me you are in need of the Master's guidance."

He seemed to loom even larger in the doorway as he leaned on his gold-handled cane and fixed Evren with a somber expression. "Wisdom is more than just the knowledge you acquire in your lessons, the skills you hone in your service. It is an integration of that knowledge with understanding and experience, knowing how your actions will affect others. Like how your actions have affected apprentice Verald, and now how they will come back to affect you."

The tall Lectern set his cane against the doorway and took a shuffling step inside the cell. "Wisdom is hard to acquire, but I believe with the Master's help, you can find it."

Swallowing the acid that rose in his throat, Evren climbed to his feet. "Yes, Lectern Uman," he replied in a dull, heavy voice. A chill settled over him, a numbness that seeped into his limbs. This was one fight he could never win.

"Then, let us pray together." Lectern Uman's strong hands went to the belt that held his robes closed.

With stiff, mechanical movements, Evren strode toward the Lectern and knelt in front of him. The coarse stone floor was rough beneath his knees, but the coldness in his gut drove all other sensations from his body.

For a moment, he toyed with the idea of throwing himself at Uman, using his weight to knock him back against the rusty nail that protruded from the door. He'd love nothing more than to see the Lectern bleeding and dying at his feet. But any attempt to retaliate or defend himself would serve no use. He could not escape what came next, and anything he did would only make his situation worse.

Lectern Uman removed his belt, heavy green and silver robe, and undertunic until he stood clad only in his thin loincloth. Evren tried not to stare at the Lectern's leg, twisted by some accident or defect of birth. Instead, he closed his eyes as the priest began to unwind the thin strips from his waist. He could not escape this horror, but he had no need to watch what the Lectern prepared to do to him.

"Lectern Uman!" An urgent voice echoed from outside the cell. A moment later, a tall figure wearing the dull green robes of an Under-Lectern appeared in the hall. "Grand Lectern Risban insists that you attend him."

"Can't you see I'm in the middle of prayers?" the Lectern snapped. Evren didn't need to open his eyes to see the anger that twisted the man's face; he'd seen it too many times as Uman "prayed" with him or one of the other apprentices.

"Forgive me, but the Grand Lectern is insistent." He dropped his voice to a whisper. "The Caliph himself has come to the Grand Chapel for the midnight service, and he has requested you by name."

"Ahh, of course." The tone of Lectern Uman's voice went from furious to pleased in an instant. "I will attend Risban at once."

Evren opened his eyes as the shuffling footsteps of the retreating Under-Lectern grew louder. Lectern Uman was bending over to retrieve

12

his robes and belt. When he straightened, he gave Evren a paternal smile. "We will continue our prayers later, apprentice."

"Yes, Lectern Uman." The words poured from Evren's mouth by rote. Another reprieve, yet the inevitable would come. Waiting would just make it worse.

The door creaked shut behind the departing Lectern, taking the light with it. Evren's heart hammered in time with the *slap, scratch* of Lectern Uman's feet. The moment the sound faded, he slumped to the ground with a shuddering gasp. Tears streamed from his eyes, and silent sobs shook his shoulders.

His mother's dying wish had been to commend him into the care of the Lecterns in the hopes that he would learn reading, writing, and everything else that made the Master's Temple the trove of wisdom in Vothmot. The Lecterns served Kiro, father of the gods, and few other priests in the city commanded as much respect.

If his mother knew the truth of what went on inside these walls, would she have condemned him to this life anyway?

His days included book learning aplenty, but far worse things besides. Things no one had told him he would have to endure—in silence, else face punishment in the form of beatings, starvation, or more abuse.

The priests claimed to serve the Master, the god of virtue and nobility. There was no virtue in the clandestine, bare-handed fights organized by the ninth-year apprentices and condoned by the Lecterns. There was no nobility in what Lectern Uman—and many other Lecterns besides—did to them in the darkness of their cells.

"Take this." Daver was suddenly beside him, pressing something hard and cold into his hand. "When he comes back—"

"Daver!" Evren's eyes widened as he stared down at the knife he gripped. A plain, utilitarian blade with a wooden handle, the sort the Lecterns used at their elaborate feasts. The sort of blades Dracat and Rhyris stole from the kitchens to throw into their sparring ring when the fighters were too evenly matched or the bout dragged on too long.

13

His eyes went to Daver. "How did you get this?" he demanded. "How did you sneak it in here?"

"With the straw." Daver pointed to their mattress.

"If the Lecterns find it, they'll—"

"Punish me?" Daver's voice went hard. "What could they do to us that they haven't already done?"

Evren had no argument for that. A day of starvation and thirst counted among the mildest of Lectern Tinis' consequences. Nothing could be worse than Lectern Uman's "prayers".

A dangerous light appeared in Daver's eyes. "When he comes back, you stick that in him and see how *he* likes it!"

"And what happens when the Lecterns find his body in our cell?" Evren demanded. "What will they do to us?"

"I don't know, and I don't care!" Daver shouted. "I just can't...do nothing!" His voice cracked, and his shoulders slumped.

Evren knew the feeling. He'd spent the last four years trapped in this nightmare. The Master's Temple was a place of learning and wisdom, and one of torment and misery. He'd tried his best to stay out of trouble, to appease Dracat, Rhyris, and the other ninth-years leading Black and Silver Towers. He'd dedicated himself to learning, tried to remain in Lectern Tinis' good graces, even volunteered for extra duties in the Grand Chapel. Yet, every time he'd thought his life was improving, something like this happened to remind him of the truth.

He couldn't live this life much longer. He'd end up beaten to death in a bare-fisted fight or succumb to madness to escape the horrors around him.

No, he had a third option.

"Then, we don't do *nothing*," he told Daver. "We do something. We escape!"

Chapter Two

"What?" Daver's eyes flew wide. "Escape?"

"It's our best hope," Evren said. He'd made up his mind the second those words left his mouth. He couldn't spend another minute in this place. "It's no worse an idea than killing Lectern Uman."

"But Evren, where would we go?"

"I don't know." Evren shook his head. "Anywhere but here."

"The Lecterns won't just let us go," Daver persisted. "They'll find us, bring us back."

"We'll run all the way across the Whispering Waste if we have to," Evren said. His mother had told stories of the vast white sand desert to the southwest of Vothmot. Surely the Lecterns couldn't reach him that far away. "We can figure it all out once we get outside, but we need to leave now, before Lectern Uman comes back. The midnight service is the shortest of the day. Even if he stretches it out to show off for the Caliph, it won't be more than an hour until he's back. I don't plan on being here, and I'm not leaving without you."

Daver's face had gone a terrified shade of pale. He might be the same age as Evren, but life's hard knocks hadn't toughened him up. He had come to the Master's Temple the sickly son of a minor Padishah of Vothmot, and though he'd recovered from the Bloody Flux, he would never be as strong as Evren—in mind or body.

"Listen, Daver," Evren said, gripping the boy's shoulder, "we've got to watch out for each other. You were going to kill Lectern Uman to save me, so there's no way I'm leaving without you. But we *have* to go now if we're going to get out. The longer we delay, the sooner we're discovered missing."

Fear and hesitation filled Daver's eyes. "But, we are…wardens of the Lecterns. Our parents gave us—"

"They gave us to the Lecterns, but that doesn't mean we're their slaves!" Evren snapped. "Come on, Daver! This can't be the life you wanted. So what if we go hungry on the streets? I'm hungry now! So what if we're cold and sleeping on hard stone? That's no better than this cell. The only difference is that out there *we* decide what we do. And we can fight back!"

Therein lay the main difference between the two of them. Evren was a fighter—even before the ninth-years dragged him into their fight ring. Daver was too scared to stand up for himself, which was why Evren had stood up for the younger boy. No one else would care for the apprentice.

"Evren, I…" Daver's voice quivered as he drew in a deep breath. "I trust you. If you think we can escape, I'm with you."

Relief washed over Evren. For a moment, he'd felt genuine fear that Daver would refuse to leave and had dreaded having to face a choice to leave his friend or stay to suffer more abuse—even now, he wasn't certain which he'd have chosen.

"Good," Evren said with a firm nod of his head. "Then we leave now. Give me your spare robe and your blanket." He rolled the items into a bundle with his own blanket and robe—his only possessions—and slipped the knife inside. The temple kitchens might not even notice its absence.

Thoughts of the kitchens made his stomach rumble, reminding him he hadn't eaten since their meager breakfast of cold oats and sliced pears.

"We'll take a detour by the kitchen and see if we can't lift a few things to keep us fed," he told Daver. "Maybe grab another knife. Never know what'll come in handy on the streets."

He had no idea what to expect outside the temple—his mother had been a seamstress, and he'd lived a comfortable, if simple life before being given to the Lecterns—but, like everything else he'd faced here in the temple, he'd adapt. Adaptability had kept him alive in every fight, even against apprentices twice his size.

"What about Seth and Wekker?" Daver asked in a quiet voice. "Are we going to leave them?"

Evren's gut clenched. The third-years were even smaller and weaker than Daver, but they were all the way across the temple in the Black Tower. "We can't get to them," he said, his heart heavy with sorrow. "Not if we're going to get out. But maybe we can come back for them another time."

"You promise?" Daver asked. His eyes fixed on Evren's face with a burning intensity.

"I promise." Evren spoke the words without hesitation. He'd say anything to get Daver out now. He could always apologize for the lie later.

He padded on sandaled feet to the door of his cell, opened it, and peered out. Lamplight flickered on bare, silent stone corridors. At this hour of the night, all of the apprentices would be in their cells. A few of the eighth- or ninth-years might be sneaking around the upper levels of the temple to take bets on tomorrow's fight—a fight he planned to miss.

"Let's go," he whispered to Daver. They crept out of the cell and shut the wooden door behind them, wincing at the groaning of the rusted hinges. The sound of quiet snoring echoed from the next cell over, and someone whimpered in another.

Evren's heart ached as he padded in silence along the corridor. He hated the thought of leaving the rest of these apprentices behind to their cruel fates, but he couldn't take them all with him. A mass escape would be far harder to obscure.

Together, he and Daver crept through the corridor, up the stairs, and into the temple proper. At this late hour, the halls were mostly empty, with the majority of the Lecterns—those not crowding into the Grand Chapel to gawk at the Caliph—either abed or devoted to late-night study.

He'd just turned toward the kitchens when a trio of green-and-silver robed Lecterns emerged from one of the temple's meditation chambers at the end of the hallway. Evren ducked back around a corner and pushed Daver against the stone wall, heart hammering. When he peered around the corner to watch their movements, a sigh of relief escaped his lips as the priests headed in the opposite direction.

If they ran into any Lecterns, he'd have to think quickly to come up with a valid explanation as to why he and Daver were roaming the temple this late at night. Perhaps he'd say that Lectern Tinis had demanded their presence to continue his reprimand. His split lip and Daver's bloodied forehead could sell the ruse well enough.

The stone corridors of the temple's main level were simply furnished, lacking the trappings of the upper floors but adorned with just enough religious statuary and ornamentation to appeal to worshippers. Oil lanterns cast soft shadows across the corridors and filled the temple with a soothing warmth—warmth that only went skin deep, never reaching the apprentices' cells below.

The smell of baking bread drifted down the hall as they approached the kitchens, and Evren's stomach growled so loud he nearly jumped. Soon, the aromas of roasted meat, potato stew, and Lectern Nallin's famous cinnamon honey loaves joined the bouquet of delicious scents. Evren swallowed the saliva that flooded his mouth and forced himself to keep his pace slow, stealthy.

He peered around the corner, his eyes scanning the lamp-lit kitchen for any sign of life. His fists clenched in frustration as he caught sight of Lectern Nallin working a ball of soft dough with a rolling pin. The Lectern whistled a pleasant tune as he applied a liberal coating of cinnamon and sugar to his loaf. A steel rack behind the balding Lectern held easily forty or fifty more loaves cooling fresh out of the oven. It took all of Evren's self-control not to rush across the kitchen and fill his pockets—he was hungry enough to eat an entire tray on his own.

Instead, he ducked below the level of the wood-topped kitchen counter and crept toward a plate of roast chicken scraps left from the Lectern's dinner. Lectern Ordari, the temple's cook, had doubtless set the discarded meat aside to feed his pet hound, but the dog would have to go hungry tonight.

Evren lifted the plate silently off the counter and held it close to his chest as he scooted back toward the door to the kitchen. Fear sparkled in Daver's dark brown eyes, but a hesitant smile broke out on his face as Evren handed him a handful of the cold poultry. Pressing a finger to his lips, Evren led the way past the kitchens.

He couldn't go out the front, not with all of the Lecterns, Under-Lecterns, and late-night temple-goers—including the Caliph's numerous entourage—between him and the double doors that led into the Court of Judgement, Vothmot's temple plaza. Even if he and Daver managed to slip through the entire temple unseen, the Wardens of the Mount, Vothmot's city guards and protectors of the Master's Temple, would stop them without hesitation.

Instead, he turned down the corridor that led toward the rear of the temple and the Gardens of Prudence.

"Where are we going?" Daver hissed in his ear.

"Trust me," he whispered back to the smaller apprentice. "I know another way out."

He'd only heard of it by chance; two eighth-years had spoken of it within his earshot as he lay dazed and recovering after a vicious bout against Athin, a Black Tower sixth-year. He'd gotten just enough information to convince him he could find it.

The corridor ended in a high-arched entrance that opened onto a marble walkway leading into the Gardens of Prudence, the Lecterns' haven of peace and meditation. At this time of night, the gardens should be empty, lit only by a few oil lanterns around the pool and seating area. No Wardens would be posted at the entrance; a wall ten paces high ringed the property to provide privacy and keep "undesirable riffraff" out.

The Gardens of Prudence were an oasis of beauty amidst the dry, dusty city of Vothmot. Lush green grass stretched three hundred paces across and thirty wide, with orange and lemon trees dotting the lawn. Bright-colored flowers grew in neat rows beside strawberry bushes, the

19

handiwork of Lectern Veros. Fountains bubbled merrily at the northern and southern corners of the lawn, and the Lecterns' sitting area—comprised of stone and wooden furniture—occupied the southwestern corner of the property.

Evren's steps led to the northeast, past the paved marble walkway that descended into the Enclave's secret tunnel. The Lecterns would inevitably search that way out, and even if he could somehow bypass the complex locking mechanisms that sealed the gate barring entrance to the passage, the tunnel ran straight and uninterrupted for half a league before letting out into the desert. That way promised only capture or death.

Instead, his steps led toward the thick hedges that lined the grassy expanse within the Gardens of Prudence. A shudder ran down his spine as he passed the diamond-shaped raised pool with its ornate stone walls, crystal clear water, and blue-tiled floor. He'd endured too many of Lectern Uman's "prayers" in its shallow depths.

He risked a glance over his shoulder and, finding the garden blessedly empty, he pushed through the hedges. Cool darkness enveloped him as the thicket obscured the glow of the flickering lamps. With only dim moonlight to see, he had to grope his way along the wall.

The sweet smell of roses came as a welcome relief. The two eighth-years had spoken of a rope ladder tucked beneath a rose bush, and this was one of the few spots in the garden where roses grew. He hissed as the thorns pricked his hands and scratched his arms, but he kept fumbling around the ground until his hands closed around hempen coils.

Metal scraped as he tugged the rope ladder free of its hiding place. The ladder had two steel hooks at one end, doubtless meant to hook onto the top of the wall, as the eighth-years had described. It took a few tries—and every *clink* of steel on stone made him wince—but finally, he got one of the ladder's hooks lodged securely.

"You go first," he told Daver. "No arguments."

Daver's mouth snapped shut, but his eyes remained wide and filled with mingled fear and apprehension. Evren refused to allow himself to fall prey to the anxiety that thrummed in the back of his mind. If he gave any thought to what happened next, how they'd survive outside the temple, he might never leave. He had to get out first, then worry about the future after.

His heart hammered a furious beat against his ribs as he watched Daver climb the rope ladder. The boy grunted and gasped with the exertion. The wall was just ten paces tall, but it felt like an hour passed before Daver finally reached the top.

"We're stuck!" Daver called down. "There's no way down the other side."

"Anchor the second hook," Evren said. "I'll figure it out when I'm up there."

When Daver had done as instructed, Evren pulled himself up the rope ladder. It proved far more difficult than he'd imagined, given the sway and sag in the knotted rope rungs. Fire coursed through legs, arms, and shoulders as he pulled himself onto the lip of the wall.

True to Daver's word, there was no way down on the far side of the wall. The faint light of the moon shone on a muddy alley bordered by buildings of crumbling brick and stone.

"Help me gather this up!" he told Daver. "This is our way down."

Together, they hauled the rope ladder up and dropped the bundle on the outside of the wall. The metal hooks *clinked* into place on the stone top of the wall, and the rope creaked as Daver clambered down slowly.

Evren's fear multiplied as he realized how exposed he was. Anyone who entered the Gardens of Prudence would spot him perched atop the wall and raise the alarm. He could do nothing more than lie flat on the stone and hope his grey apprentice robes were too dull to be visible.

A squelching *thump* echoed below him, and he glanced down to see Daver sprawled on the muddy ground of the alley. Quick as Lectern Ityer's pet mongoose, Evren hurried down the ladder.

"You hurt?" he asked, crouching beside Daver.

"No," the younger boy said. "I just lost my footing on…that."

Evren recoiled from the shape Daver indicated. A corpse, silent and still. It lay facing the wall, so he couldn't tell if it had been a man or woman. The stink filling the alley made it clear the corpse had gone undisturbed for days. At least that meant few people other than the ninth-year apprentices came this way.

He tried in vain to dislodge the hooks holding the rope ladder in place but gave up after a few futile attempts. They needed to put as much distance between them and the temple as possible before Lectern Uman discovered their absence.

He helped Daver to his feet then hesitated, uncertain what to do now. The alley ran for twenty paces to the north and south, bordered by the temple walls and the backs of the crumbling buildings, then connected into more of the narrow back streets that fed into the environs around the Court of Judgement.

He had no idea where to go, but he didn't care. He was free of the Master's Temple, free of their torment. He'd exchange all the uncertainty on Einan for his freedom any day.

Chapter Three

"Can't…keep…running!" Daver panted from twenty paces behind him.

Evren ground his teeth but slowed his speed. "We'll take a break, but we've got to keep moving."

With a gasp, Daver collapsed onto the staircase of a crumbling stone house and lay panting. Evren remained standing, controlling his breathing, and forced himself not to snap at Daver. They'd been running for less than ten minutes, so they couldn't have put more than a few streets between them and the Master's Temple. He'd have to get much farther from the Court of Judgement before he would begin to feel safe.

Problem was, the few scraps of food he'd filched from the kitchens hadn't given him much energy. Between the day's labors, the fight with Verald, and the exertion from climbing the ladder, he was reaching the end of his limited supply of strength. He needed more food, water, and rest.

But not yet.

"Just a few minutes," he told Daver. "We need to get as far as we can before they come looking for us." Neither of them needed a reminder of what would happen if the Lecterns caught up with them.

He racked his mind for a plan. They could always go back to the house where he'd lived with his mother in the Crafter's District far to the west of Vothmot. No, the Lecterns would look there first. To be safe, they ought to head in the opposite direction. That meant east toward the

Ward of Bliss. Though he'd never seen the kaffehouses of Vothmot with their bright-colored wooden signs depicting steaming wooden mugs and nude bodies, he'd heard the eighth- and ninth-years boasting about their many visits. The maze-like alleyways behind the kaffehouses ought to provide plenty of places for them to hide.

"Let's go." He reached out a hand to help Daver up. "We've got to keep moving."

Daver groaned as he stood. "Where are we going?"

"To the Ward of Bliss."

Daver's eyebrows shot up. "Why?"

"Lots of twisty alleys where we can get lost," Evren told him. "Or lose anyone chasing us."

"Okay," Daver said. Despite the worry in his large eyes, the boy's voice held a quiet trust. Evren felt the burden of caring for the smaller apprentice weighing heavy on his shoulders, but he bore it as he had for the last three years. Everyone needed someone to watch their back—he'd watch Daver's, just as he wished he had someone to watch his.

Nearly a quarter-league and dozens of patrols separated them from the Ward of Bliss. Three times in the space of half an hour, Evren had to drag a tired Daver into a muddy side alley to wait until the mirror-armored Wardens passed. Every delay added to the tightness in his gut. At any moment, Lectern Uman would discover their absence and raise the alarm. Before daybreak, the Wardens would be searching for them. They had to get off the streets as soon as possible.

But it wasn't long before Evren began to feel his own strength flagging. The rush of adrenaline brought on by their escape had faded long ago, and only determination drove him onward. Grim resolve couldn't soothe the aches in his pummeled body, fill his growling stomach, or shield him from the night's chill. He knew he had to get somewhere warm, quiet, and safe before he collapsed.

To his relief, he found the Prime Bazaar silent and still. During the day, Vothmot's main marketplace was a bustle of activity. Camels, horses, mules, and oxen hauled goods and passengers in and out of the city. Merchants hawked their wares of trinkets, clothing, fabrics, and food.

Treasure-hunters and fortune-seekers flocked to Vothmot in the hopes of finding the fabled lost city of Enarium, said to be hidden in the Empty Mountains north of the city.

Yet now, the wood-and-canvas stalls were closed, the livestock stabled, and the merchants abed. As he and Daver scurried around the fringes of the marketplace, he saw only two people: a bald, bearded man and a pale-skinned southerner, both wearing the garb of mountaineers. With their attention focused on their train of mountain mules, they didn't seem to see Evren or Daver.

The tension in Evren's shoulders faded as he caught sight of a dark alleyway just beyond the Prime Bazaar. He ducked into the cramped lane without hesitation. The squelching mud under his slippered feet and the thick reek of offal came as a welcome relief; anything to get him out of sight and away from the inevitable pursuit.

He gripped Daver's hand and worked his way deeper into the alleys, the dim moonlight guiding his footsteps. He didn't slow until he had left the Prime Bazaar far behind and all but lost his way in the twisting, turning, narrow lanes of the Ward of Bliss.

Finally, he allowed himself to slow. An open doorway to his right beckoned, and Evren ducked inside warily. Loud snoring came from the far end of the room, so Evren slipped into the empty shadows against the wall behind the door. No one could see him and Daver from the alley, and he'd hear any searchers coming before they spotted him. Right now, given his exhaustion, that was the best sort of shelter he could hope for.

The door shielded most of the stiff breeze that drifted through the alley but failed to keep out the chill in the air. Evren unrolled their little bundle and handed Daver a blanket and spare robe. He took one for himself and used it to wrap as much of his body as the threadbare cloth could cover. Huddled against Daver, he could almost stop shivering…almost.

He clutched the knife in his right hand. The feel of solid wood and steel reassured him. He might be cold, hungry, and afraid, but that was far preferable to anything that awaited him back in the Master's Temple.

* * *

The sound of heavy booted feet reached Evren's ears, and he awoke in an instant, his grip on his knife tightening. Life in the temple had turned him into a light sleeper—he never knew when one of the Lecterns would visit for late-night or early-morning "prayers".

The tension faded from his shoulders as he spotted the source of the noise. A drunk staggered into the crumbling building, carrying a clay bottle that sloshed blue liquid onto his already soiled shirt and splattered his boots. It would have stained his pants had he been wearing any, but he seemed to have lost them somewhere along his teetering way. He didn't notice the two of them huddled in their blankets behind the door. Instead, he took two unsteady steps then collapsed to the stone floor with a loud *whomph*.

Evren winced as the drunk's face hit the stone—hard. The pain of the man's crushed nose and split lip would give the inevitable hangover a run for its imperials. The movement reminded Evren of his own injuries. His lip had swollen to three times its size and sent a twinge through his face anytime he moved.

He glanced around at their temporary refuge. The building was one of the older constructions in Vothmot, as evidenced by the rotting wood and crumbling clay bricks. Modern builders used the grey and red stone hauled from the Empty Mountains or bricks pressure-molded rather than oven-fired. The wooden floor beams had sagged, cracked, or simply rotted away, leaving gaping holes at various intervals around the building's interior. Only the Mistress' luck had kept Evren from falling into one a few paces away from the door through which he'd entered the previous night.

It might be a withered husk of a building, but it still felt better than their cold cell in the Master's Temple.

"Daver," he whispered and shook the boy asleep on his shoulder. "Get up."

"Wha--?" Daver jerked upright with a loud snort. He blinked a few times and rubbed the sleep from his eyes and seemed confused by their surroundings. "Where are we?"

"By its looks, I'd say an abandoned house somewhere in the Ward of Bliss, not too far from the Prime Bazaar."

"Oh." Daver's face fell, as if his mind had just registered the reason for his being here.

"Come on. Let's get up and head to the Bazaar."

"Why?" Daver asked, his face wrinkling.

"We might be able to beg a few coins," Evren said. On his few visits with his mother to the Prime Bazaar, he'd seen his fair share of beggars—boys, girls, old men and women, and everything in between. Wealthy southerners on pilgrimage to the Master's Temple would often put coins into their begging bowls; doubtless it made them feel more devout, or at least appear that way. If he and Daver could reach the Bazaar before the crowd of beggars, he might be able to get enough coins to buy breakfast. He'd have a clearer head after he got something in his stomach.

"Are you sure that's a good idea?" Daver asked. "If the Lecterns are already looking for us—"

"One of us can keep watch while the other one asks for coins." Evren studied Daver up and down. "You'll probably be better doing the begging." The smaller boy looked a pathetic sight, with his bloodied forehead, gaunt features, scrawny frame, and threadbare apprentice robes.

"Just keep this out of sight." He tucked Daver's crescent moon pendant beneath his collar and out of sight. "We look ragged enough already, but a bit of mud should help." To emphasize his point, he scooped up a handful of the muck the drunk had tracked in on his boots and rubbed it onto his face and clothing. His senses recoiled from the reek, but he did his best to ignore it as he applied a coat of dirt to Daver's face. It would be all the camouflage they'd have for now.

Daver followed him through the alleys into the Prime Bazaar. At this early hour, few merchants had opened their stalls and only a trickle of people wandered through the marketplace. A single caravan rode past, treasure-hunters doubtless intending to get an early start on their trek through the Empty Mountains.

Evren planted Daver on a corner where the main avenue through Vothmot connected with the road to the North Gate.

"Hold out your hand, and do your best to sound as pitiful as you look, eh?" He gave Daver a smile, which sent throbbing pain through his healing lip. "I'll be nearby watching for Lecterns. We leave the moment you get enough coin for breakfast."

The sun peeked its golden face over the eastern horizon, bathing Evren with welcome warmth as he took up position on the corner opposite Daver. His vantage offered a clear view of the avenue that led through the Prime Bazaar toward the Court of Judgement. If any Lecterns or Wardens came from that way, he'd see them first.

The flow of traffic began to increase as more merchants, wagoneers, and fortune-seekers crowded into the Prime Bazaar. The Mistress' luck smiled on them, and within ten minutes, a grey-haired man in the rough-spun tunic and cloak of a pilgrim deposited a coin in Daver's outstretched hand. He'd barely shuffled up the street before Daver leapt to his feet and ran toward Evren.

"Look!" he said, excitement sparkling in his eyes. "A whole silver half-drake."

Evren's heart leapt. "That's enough for a good meal, a change of clothes, and some shoes!"

"No it ain't," came a quiet voice from behind Evren. "That's enough to earn you a beating instead of a knifing."

Evren's gut clenched at the menace in the words. He spun to meet the threat and found himself face-to-face with a tall, dark-haired boy.

The youth wore clothes far filthier and more ragged than Evren's own, and his black hair stuck out at wild angles from his head, forming an erratic halo around his angular face. He stared down his hawkish nose at Evren. "Big mistake, angling on our turf." He stuck out a muddy hand. "Hand it over, and I'll tell my lads to take it easy on you."

Evren spotted three smaller, equally mud-stained and disheveled boys hovering behind. They looked at least a year or two younger than the speaker, who had to be around Evren's own age.

"No," Evren said. He took the coin from Daver and held it in a clenched fist. "This is ours, but you can have your turf back. We're just—"

"Just trespassing is what you're doing." The boy took a threatening step closer, towering a full hand's breadth taller than Evren. "Either hand it over, or my boys and I will cut off your hand, then pry it from your severed fingers."

The words were doubtless meant as a threat, but Evren felt no fear. He'd been threatened by youths far larger and tougher.

"You're welcome to try," he snarled in a low voice. "But it might not turn out like you expect."

A knife suddenly appeared in the boy's hand, and he pressed the tip under Evren's chin. "You sure about that?"

Evren raised an eyebrow. "What, you're going to kill me here? In the middle of the Prime Bazaar?"

"No." The boy smiled, revealing two missing incisors. "I'm going to drag you into the alleyway and kill you there."

Two of the smaller boys grabbed Evren's arms, and he allowed them to push him past the street tough, around a corner, and down the alley. His teeth clenched as he heard Daver cry out, but he knew he was the target for their punishment. They'd only beat on Daver once they finished with him—they had to break the stronger of the two in order to send a message. These street toughs were a lot like the eighth and ninth-year apprentices.

Well, there was one real difference. They were Evren's size or smaller, and they had no idea what he could do.

The moment he was out of sight of the Prime Bazaar, he moved. He jerked his right arm up, tearing it free of his captor's grip, and drove the tip of his elbow into the boy's nose. A loud *crunch* echoed as the boy cried out and clapped a hand to his nose. Evren brought his right fist

29

whipping across his body and drove it into his other captor's stomach, right beneath the ribs. The boy gave a loud "ugghh" and doubled over.

The oldest street tough's eyes went wide as he saw his two comrades fall. Evren drew back his fist and lashed out with a powerful punch that caught the bigger boy in the jaw. The dark-haired youth sagged, his head reeling. Evren cleared the distance to Daver's captor in two quick shuffling steps and brought him down with a quick jab and an uppercut to the chin.

"You hurt?" he asked Daver.

"No, but—" Daver's eyes flew wide and locked onto something behind Evren.

Evren ducked and spun in one smooth motion, and the dark-haired boy's balled fist sailed over his head. Before the street tough could recover, Evren drove a quick punch into his kidney, then another into his liver. The boy fell back against the wall with a groan.

Evren whipped out his knife and pressed it to the boy's throat. "You sure you want to keep trying to take my coin?"

The dark-haired boy blinked to clear his eyes then froze as he felt the steel against his neck. "No!" he said, careful not to move. "Coin's yours."

"Thank you." Evren removed the knife but didn't sheath it. He backed toward Daver, never taking his eyes off the street tough. "Now, if there's nothing else, my friend and I will be on our way."

"How about you join us?" the boy asked.

The question caught Evren by surprise, and he nearly stumbled. "What?"

"Join us." The boy gave Evren another gap-toothed grin. "Fists like yours'll come in right handy when facing the other crews. And that knife of yours is mighty nice."

Evren glanced down at the wooden-handled knife Daver had stolen from the temple kitchens, then at the rusted blade the dark-haired boy had dropped. His knife seemed a weapon of legend by comparison.

"Join your crew?" he asked. "A crew of thieves?"

"Thieves, beggars, pickpockets, whatever we need to be." Again, with the beaming smile that showed too-few teeth. "How we make our coin's less important than the fact that we make it. We've got warm beds, food in our bellies—or at least, some food, provided Porky here don't eat it all."

One of the smaller boys, a rotund lad who barely reached Evren's shoulders, blushed.

"And you want the two of us?" Evren asked.

"Well, the invite's for you," the street tough said, "but if you two are joined at the hip—"

"We are." Evren's voice left no doubt. "He comes with me, or no dice."

"Fair enough, I suppose." The dark-haired youth stroked his scruffy, fuzz-covered chin. "So long as he makes enough coin to pay his way, he'll fit in well enough."

Evren hesitated. Until a few hours ago, he'd been an apprentice, training to be a priest at the most respected temple for a thousand leagues. Now, he was going to be a thief? Anything was better than the horrors that awaited him in the Master's Temple.

"Deal," he said, thrusting out a hand.

The dark-haired youth eyed it, then shook his head. "Nuh-uh. The offer's mine to make, but the final decision ain't. You want in, we've got to take you to the Warren to see the Red Grinner."

Chapter Four

"And who might you be?" asked the Red Grinner, a boy who couldn't be more than a year older than Evren.

"Says his name's Evren," Tomaz replied.

"That so?" He studied Evren from head to toe, then his eyes went to the dark-haired street tough. "Another stray to join our fold, Tomaz?"

Tomaz nodded. "Stray he might be, Swain, but he's got teeth and a nasty bite."

The Red Grinner grinned. "Is that why the three of you look like you've pounded your face on every paving stone between here and the Court of Judgement?"

Here, turned out to be an abandoned three-story, stone building in the Ward of Bliss, a stone's throw from the back entrance into Divinity House. The upper levels had begun to crumble from neglect, but the walls and ground floor had been built to last. Some of the wooden doors had even survived scavengers, and a few of the cheaper items of furniture remained intact.

The Red Grinner lounged on a stuffed armchair with frayed upholstery and sagging cushions, yet he treated it like a royal throne. The other boys around him, none older than fifteen or sixteen, gave Swain the sort of deference the boys of Grey Tower had treated Rhyris. Swain was the leader of this little crew—no more than ten or fifteen youths, from what Evren could see.

Not a very imposing leader, either, at least not compared to some of the opponents Evren had faced in the Master's Temple. Swain was the same height and build as Evren, with matted black hair that hung in thick dreadlocks down his back. Not even his mother would have called him handsome, with his flattened nose, wide jaw, close-set eyes, and thick forehead. His threadbare clothes bore the same mud, food, and drink stains as the others. On his belt hung a double-bladed hunting knife, the handle made with silver-inlaid wood—the mark of his status.

"He don't look like much," Swain said after a moment. "And his pal looks one good blow away from crumbling."

"Looks can be deceiving." Evren stepped in front of Daver. The smaller boy had grown more and more nervous with every second they spent in this place, and his eyes darted between the street toughs scattered around the building's interior. "You want to come and find out for yourself?"

Even though his insides churned, he kept his exterior calm and hard. His many fights had taught him to never show fear. Fear put a weapon in your opponent's hand and gave him the advantage.

"You want to fight *me*?" Swain raised an eyebrow, and his tone held a mocking edge. "Do you know why they call me the Red Grinner? It's on account of the smile I give my enemies." He slashed a finger across his throat for emphasis.

"How terrifying," Evren said, his tone dry. "I'm sure you spent a lot of sleepless nights trying to come up with it."

Swain's eyes narrowed and his expression hardened. Evren tensed in expectation of a fight, his fists clenching. Provoking an enemy had worked in the past, as their anger made them act rashly. He'd be ready when Swain charged. Though if the Red Grinner brought out his knife, he'd be in trouble.

To his surprise, Swain broke into a laugh. "You're right, Tomaz. He does have bite."

The stiffness drained from Tomaz' posture and a tentative grin touched his lips.

Swain clapped the dark-haired youth on the back. "Tomaz may not be much of a thief or pickpocket, but he knows his way around a dust-up. It's why I allow him to run his own crew rather than working alone. He says you've got the goods, so I'm willing to give you a shot at joining up. What do you say?"

Evren glanced back at Daver. The smaller boy no longer looked terrified, but his fear hadn't gone entirely. He needed to protect Daver, and if that meant joining a crew of street toughs to earn enough coin for food, clothing, and shelter, so be it. He had skills enough for both of them.

"What's the catch?" His eyes returned to Swain. "This isn't out of the goodness of your heart, so what do you want from us?"

"A share of your take." Swain grinned. "Two out of every five coins you earn goes to me. For the upkeep of our little palace, of course."

Judging by the filthy lengths of canvas hanging from the windows and the dust covering every surface, not a lot of coin went into that upkeep.

"And," Swain continued, "if we get in a dust-up with one of the other crews that run in the area, you fight for us." He thrust out a hand. "We got a deal?"

A percentage of his earnings—earnings he had no idea how he'd make—plus the requirement that he'd fight for them. This new life had a lot in common with his life in the Master's Temple, though at least out here he'd have a shred of control over who he fought, when, and why. And out here, Lectern Uman couldn't touch him.

"Deal." Evren shook Swain's hand.

Swain studied Daver up and down. "With a bit of effort, we'll turn you into quite the beggar boy," he said with a grin. Quick as striking lightning, the Red Grinner pulled back his fist and punched Daver hard in the face. Daver's head snapped back, and he fell to the ground with a cry.

Evren lashed out at Swain, but strong arms dragged him backward before he could land a blow.

"Easy, easy!" A vicious light twinkled in Swain's eyes as he raised his hands. "I ain't gonna hurt him for real. Just polishing him up a bit, making him look the part." A cruel smile twisted his lips. "Black eyes do wonders to open the pilgrims' purses."

Evren struggled in his captors' grip, but they were taller and stronger.

Swain took a step back and eyed Evren. "Consider this his initiation into the crew. That gonna be a problem, new guy?"

With effort, Evren clamped down on the anger burning in his gut. "No," he said between clenched teeth.

"Good." Swain nodded, and the two boys released his arms.

Evren rushed to Daver, who still lay dazed on the ground. Blood trickled from the smaller boy's nose and his right eye had begun to purple. Evren gritted his teeth. If Swain raised a hand against Daver again, they *would* have a real problem—one that could only end in a fight.

Evren dabbed at Daver's nose with the sleeve of his apprentice robes, then helped him stand.

"But before you join," Swain said, "there's a little matter of entry payment."

Evren's heart sank. Of course that wouldn't be the end of it.

"Everyone in my crew's got to pull their own weight." Swain gestured around him. "You want to join, you bring proof that you're worth accepting."

Evren's hand tightened around the coin he'd stuffed into his pocket. Though Tomaz hadn't mentioned it to Swain, Evren hated the idea of giving it up. He needed it to buy food, water, and shoes—three things he couldn't do without in this new life of his.

Swain's eyes went to Daver. "I think I'll take that." His finger indicated the platinum crescent moon pendant around the boy's neck, which had spilled from his as he fell. "The trinket ought to be worth something."

Daver's hand went to the pendant and his fingers closed around it. He treasured it far more than Evren ever had.

Evren stepped forward quickly. "Let him keep his and take mine instead." He lifted his necklace over his head and held it out to Swain.

Swain snatched it and studied the scrap of jewelry. He seemed not to recognize the shape and inscription for what it was. Few outside the Master's Temple would. That was for the best. Evren wanted nothing to connect him back to the Lecterns. He wanted freedom from the reminders of the horrors he'd faced every day of his apprenticeship, but that wasn't the only reason. His interaction with Swain made it clear that the boy would turn him over to the Lecterns without hesitation if it earned him a few coins.

"Done." Swain pocketed the pendant and gave a dismissive wave. "Tomaz, find them a place to bunk, and give them the lay of the land."

"Will do, Swain." Tomaz turned to Evren and Daver. "This way."

Evren shot a glance at Swain, who had returned to his ragged armchair throne and now sat like an imperious, mud-covered monarch. The vicious light hadn't left the boy's eyes. Evren understood why Swain had become the leader, even of boys older and stronger than him. The cruelest, most ruthless always attained power.

Tomaz led them through a pair of hanging canvas "doors" and into a cramped space along the eastern wall of the building.

"We ain't got much in the way of blankets or beds," Tomaz told them. "Those you've got will be a start, but if you want to be warm at night, you'll need to steal some more. I can point you in the direction of a few merchants who pay more attention to their purses and less to their wares, if you'd like."

"Thank you." Evren nodded. "Where can we get some food and water?"

Tomaz shrugged. "Anything you want, you beg or swipe." He lowered his voice. "Save that coin of yours for when you really need it. Like a day when no one's giving, or you're too hungry or tired to steal. Trust me, you'll want it handy to get Swain off your back. When he gets into one of his moods…" His gaze darted to Daver's black eye. "Just keep it somewhere safe for a bad day. This life has more of them than you'd expect."

* * *

Evren felt safer as he followed Tomaz into the Prime Bazaar once more. The bustling mid-morning traffic would hide him from any searching Wardens or Lecterns, and he could always cut back into the narrow lanes to lose pursuers.

On Swain's orders, Tomaz was giving them a basic primer to the life of a street thief.

"The Bazaar's a good place to lift purses, but you've got to have quick hands and quicker feet," Tomaz said in a low voice. "It's thick with Warden patrols, and lots of the merchants have their own guards to protect their wares. Some actually hire men to pretend to shop, then pounce on us if we try to filch anything. You gotta be ready to run in an instant, even if that means abandoning your loot."

The look he shot at Daver spoke volumes—"and your friend" it meant, even if he didn't say the words aloud.

"Now," Tomaz continued, "if you're looking for wares—blankets, trinkets to re-sell, clothing, and so on—your best bet is to leave the Prime Bazaar." He pointed down the main avenue toward the eastern gate. "The smaller merchants set up in the Summer Market, where it's cheaper to set up a stall and there's less competition with the ones who run the Bazaar. They're the ones who can't afford to hire guards, and the Warden patrols don't pass as often. If you wait until the merchants' backs are turned or they're with a customer, you ought to be able to lift something small nice and easy."

Tomaz led them away from the Prime Bazaar and down the main avenue. Ten streets closer to the eastern gate, a smaller marketplace bordered both sides of the broad thoroughfare. The stalls were smaller and less colorful than those crowding the Prime Bazaar, the quality of the merchandise of lower quality.

"There's where you go for blankets and cloth." Tomaz pointed to a row of stalls where colorful but faded bolts of fabric and woven blankets were proudly displayed. "Those merchants are sharp-eyed enough that you'll have to wait until the streets are really full before trying anything. But if you time it right, you can get away clean."

Mid-morning traffic in the Summer Market hadn't yet reached its peak, but enough people surged up and down the broad avenue that Evren didn't have to worry about Warden patrols spotting them.

"You can find water at any horse trough in the Ward of Bliss or Prime Bazaar, if you don't mind sharing with a few animals. Food's down that way." Tomaz indicated a section of stalls where merchants hawked fresh fruits, vegetables, dates, figs, honey, dried meat, and the flatbread that was a staple of the Vothmot diet. "Stick with the small stuff, anything you can fit in your pockets." He shot Evren a grin. "Porky once tried to make off with a pair of melons. Let's just say that did *not* end well, either for Porky or the fruit."

Evren tried to smile back, but he couldn't summon the energy. He was too hungry and thirsty for pleasantries, his anger at Swain hadn't yet dimmed, and the wealth of information on street thieving overwhelmed him. It was just so much all at once.

Tomaz clapped him on the back. "Don't worry, Evren. You'll get used to it soon enough." His smile wavered. "Hunger's a quick teacher."

Evren nodded. "I'll make it work," he said with more confidence than he felt.

"You better." Tomaz' gaze pierced Evren. "I vouched for you, so it'll be on me if you don't. I got my own boys to worry about." With those words, he turned and ran up the street, back toward the Prime Bazaar and his waiting crew.

Evren glanced over at Daver. The black eye made his face seem even paler than usual, and his gaze darted around nervously. No way he'd pull off any thieving today. The smaller boy would need more time to get used to his new life. That meant the burden fell on Evren—again.

"Stay here," he told Daver, "watch for the Wardens. I'm going to get us something to eat."

Daver nodded. "S-Sure," he stammered. He looked a few seconds from collapse. Maybe they could use that.

"Better yet, sit over there and try to get us a few more coins."
Evren pointed to a bare patch of dusty ground beside the avenue. A
nearby cloth merchant's stall would offer Daver some shade, but he sat
far enough away that hopefully he wouldn't piss off the merchant or the
beggar fifty paces up the street.

Once Daver was situated, Evren slipped into the flow of traffic and
headed toward the section of stalls where Tomaz had told him he'd find
food. His eyes roamed over the flatbread, the fresh fruits and vegetables,
the dried meat, and the heaping piles of nuts, dried fruit, dates, and
olives—an abundance that, as with his life in the temple, lay ever out of
his reach.

But the rules of his apprenticeship to the Lecterns no longer bound
him. He could take what he wanted if he was clever and quick enough.

He'd never considered himself a thief, but he'd had his fair share of
practice swiping food from the temple kitchens. This couldn't be that
much different. He simply had to stay unnoticed, wait until the food was
unguarded, then make his move. Instead of portly Lectern Nallin, he'd
have to watch out for a merchant. The open-air market had many more
avenues of escape than the darkened corridors of the Master's Temple.
How hard could it be?

His heart hammered as he sidled toward a cart heaped high with
dates. He'd gotten within two paces of the cart when someone jostled
him from the side, sending him stumbling forward. He caught himself on
the edge of the stall, but before he could move, a strong hand snapped
out to close around his wrist.

"Not again, you don't!"

Chapter Five

The hand on Evren's wrist was gnarled and twisted by rheumatism, and it belonged to an equally gnarled and twisted man easily in his sixth or seventh decade. His left knee, visible beneath the hem of his dull brown robe, was swollen to three times its normal size. Yet, when Evren tried to break free of the man's grasp, he found surprising strength in his captor's grip.

"You young miscreants have stolen from my stall five times this week already!" the old man shouted down at him, anger in his dark eyes. "No more, by the Apprentice." He scanned the crowd as if searching for a Warden to flag down.

"I'm no thief!" Evren protested. "I was just walking by when someone bumped into me. I was just stopping myself from falling. Check my pockets, I haven't taken anything."

The merchant patted him down roughly and grunted when he found Evren's knife and coin. "What do you have to say about this?"

"They're mine." Evren shook his head. "I didn't steal either of them." It wasn't quite a lie. The coin had been given to Daver, and the smaller boy had been the one to take the knife from the temple kitchens.

"You expect me to believe that?" the man snapped. "I could just call the Wardens over and—"

Evren tried to break free again. "No! I'm not a thief." He wasn't, yet.

The man's eyes narrowed. "Is that so?"

Evren nodded. "Yes."

"So you expect me to believe you're an honest lad?"

"As honest as a Lectern!" The man would only know of the priests' reputation, not the truth of what went on behind the temple's closed doors.

The old man's expression hardened. "Then, what's a lad like you doing here in the Summer Market begging for coin?" He thrust a twisted finger at Daver. "I saw you come in here with him."

"Aye, I did," Evren said, thinking quickly. "He's my…brother. We lost our parents to the Bloody Flux a week back, and we've no other family to take us in. Life on the streets has been hard." Daver's black eye, bloodied forehead, and still-healing lip ought to sell the lie. "I figured my brother might make a few coins this way, get us something to eat while I looked for work."

"It's work you're looking for?" One bushy white eyebrow climbed near to the top of the man's bald head.

"It is, sir." Evren adopted his most sincere tone, the same one he used when accepting Lectern Tinis' admonitions. "My father taught me to read, write, and do sums, and I know my way around grooming a horse." All skills he'd picked up doing chores in the Master's Temple.

The old man snorted. "Not much call for any of that around here." He gestured to the merchant stalls beside his. "None of us earn enough to require bookkeeping, and we're too busy trying to scrape together a living to bother with reading or writing. But I could use a pair of hands to help me unload my wares and load them at the end of the day. You look strong enough to merit twenty copper bits for a day of work. Think you'd be up for it?"

The offer surprised Evren. "Absolutely!" he said before the man changed his mind. Right now, he'd do anything to avoid attracting attention. Doubtless the Lecterns had discovered his empty cell, and they'd involved the Wardens in the hunt for him and Daver. He had to be as unremarkable and unobtrusive as possible. Evren the hard-working orphan boy was far less interesting than Evren the escaped apprentice.

"Think your brother'd be up for some work as well?" The old man rubbed his white-stubbled chin with a gnarled hand. "He doesn't look quite as strong as you, but I figure he'll do enough work to earn the two of you a decent lunch. Sound fair?"

Evren cast a glance toward Daver. The smaller apprentice made a pathetic enough figure that they'd probably earn more coins begging, but it could end up attracting the Wardens' attention. "Throw in a pair of copper bits for him, and you've got yourself a deal."

The old man's eyes narrowed. "Think you can negotiate, do you?" He pursed his lips, which deepened the lines around his mouth. "For fifty years I've been setting up shop here, and never once has anyone gotten the better end of a bargain."

"First time for everything, I suppose." Evren shrugged. "Unless you'd rather do the hauling yourself."

The white-haired man stared hard at him for a long moment, then smiled. "Good to see you've got some brains in that head of yours." He held out a gnarled hand. "Folks around here call me Kaltris."

"Evren." Evren shook the man's hand, gently. He'd seen how painful Lectern Hobell's rheumatism could be. "My brother's Daver."

"Well met, Evren. Fetch your brother over, and I'll show you what needs moving." A sly smile stretched the old man's wrinkled face. "You may have gotten a few extra coins out of me, but I intend to make you earn every one of them."

* * *

Evren groaned as he set the last of the heavy crates onto the wagon. He sat on the large wheel and leaned back against the side of the cart, basking in the warmth and brilliance of the setting sun. It felt good to sit after hours of hard labor. True to his word, Kaltris had made him earn those coins. At last count, he'd unloaded nearly fifty wooden crates filled with figs, tart yellow lemons, dates, pomegranates, sweet peaches, and plums. He doubted he'd ever get the stink of garlic off his hands, clothes, and face, and the sweat drenching his tunic reeked from the sack of half-rotten onions that had spilled all over him.

Daver had done his best to help, but most of the crates had been too heavy for him to lift. Thankfully, Jodech, one of Kaltris' fellow fruit peddlers, had needed help sorting apples, so Daver had spent the day sitting on a stool in the shade.

Evren wiped his streaming forehead and turned back toward Kaltris' stall.

"Give us a hand here," Kaltris called. The old merchant was struggling with the canvas that provided a roof for his wooden stand. Evren hurried over to help him, and together they unhooked it from the roof beams and rolled it into a tight bundle, which Evren hauled over to Kaltris' cart. As he set it down, the heavy roll knocked over a wooden crate, spilling apricots all over the interior of the wagon.

Evren tensed in expectation of a scolding from Kaltris—if something like this had happened in the Master's Temple, the Lecterns would have slapped him with a week of extra chores, and Lectern Uman would have paid him a visit in his cell. The dull chill seeped into his body as he stared at the merchant. But to his surprise, Kaltris didn't snap, bark, or shout.

"No matter," Kaltris said with a wave of his hand. "Damned crate was about to break anyway. Just get the apricots into the one with the plums. But mind your feet. Last thing I need is more crushed fruit!"

Evren swallowed his surprise and scrambled up onto the wagon to clean up the mess. The merchant's reaction seemed so odd, so kind, compared to everything he'd experienced the last five years in the Master's Temple.

When he finished cleaning up and jumped down from the wagon, Kaltris handed him a wineskin. "It's a cheap Vothmot vintage that's mostly water by now, but it ought to be better than nothing."

With a grateful nod, Evren took a long gulp. He grimaced at the tart, vinegar-tasting wine—the Lecterns would murder anyone who served them this sort of swill—but swallowed it anyway. It was better than drinking from a horse trough.

"Your payment, as promised." Kaltris held out a handful of small coins. "Twenty-two copper bits. Your brother's got your food."

Evren counted the coins at a glance; he'd always had a head for numbers. Kaltris had given him twenty-four copper bits. Hesitation warred within him. Pocket the coins or tell the merchant of the error? Two bits could buy him and Daver a decent meal or a spare tunic.

After a moment, he sighed and held out the two extra copper bits. "You gave me too many." Kaltris had treated him with decency; he hadn't had a lot of that in his life. He might have joined a crew of thieves, but he couldn't bring himself to steal from the old merchant. "Our deal was twenty-two, not twenty-four."

"I know. What sort of idiot merchant would I be if I couldn't keep a proper count?" Kaltris' sly smile returned. "I wanted to see for myself what manner of lad you are."

Evren's eyebrows rose. It had been a test? "Why?"

"Because I need someone strong to help run my business," Kaltris said. "Never had sons of my own, no one to lend a hand with the things I can't do." He held up his hands. "Rheumatism's getting worse. More pain, less mobility. Soon enough, I won't be able to get out of a chair unaided. Last thing an old man wants is to face death by starvation because his body's turned against him."

Evren could understand that. Lectern Hobell had a pair of apprentices to serve as his full-time caretakers. He couldn't even feed himself and needed help to use the chamber pot or turn over in bed.

"I've been watching you all day," Kaltris continued. "You and your brother both. You work hard without complaint, and you're smart enough to learn what I have to teach you. Now, it turns out you're more honest than most men I've met. My business, what little there is, would be in good hands. If you're willing, I'd like to take you with me on my trip to Mountainfall, day after next. Show you the ropes."

Evren hesitated. Life in the Master's Temple had taught him to be wary of everything—any small gesture of goodwill could conceal ulterior motives, deceit, or abuse. He wanted to believe Kaltris. He'd seen nothing to indicate the man would harm him or Daver. And, a trip to the village of Mountainfall, two days' ride to the southeast, would get him out of Vothmot and away from the Lecterns.

"Yes," he said after a moment. "I'll collect our things, and Daver and I will be—"

"No." Kaltris' face darkened. "The offer's only for you."

A fist squeezed Evren's gut. "What?"

Kaltris sighed. "This business can barely feed me, and I'm taking a gamble by bringing you on. There's no way I could feed the both of you." Sorrow filled his eyes. "I need a strong lad, and your brother…isn't. I'm sorry, but I can only afford one. You."

Evren's heart sank. It had been too much to hope for, hadn't it? Life was too cruel to give him anything good.

"I know it's a big ask," Kaltis continued in a quiet voice. "Leaving your brother like that. But I had to make the offer anyway. Sleep on it. Come back here tomorrow, and if the answer's a no, I'll understand."

Evren opened his mouth to say he already had an answer, but no words came out. He felt responsible for protecting Daver. No way he could leave the smaller apprentice with Red Grinner and his crew. Yet, a part of him ached to go with Kaltris and leave his life behind.

"I'll…think about it," he said finally.

Kaltris nodded. "Good." He groaned loudly and his joints clicked as he climbed onto the stiff-backed wooden seat of his cart. "Until tomorrow, Evren." A snap of the traces set his old, dull-eyed mule into motion, and the cart rumbled down the avenue.

Evren watched the cart until it disappeared around a corner, and his heart grew heavy. His eyes went to Daver, who still sat on the stool where he'd spent the day sorting produce. The smaller apprentice was busy stuffing flatbread into his mouth, alternating bites with the juicy peach in his hand. Daver wouldn't survive on the streets without him.

He strode over to the seated boy. "Come on, Daver. Let's get back before nightfall."

"Here, this is your share." Daver handed him a piece of flatbread, a small strip of dried meat, and a peach. He stood, brushed the crumbs from his robes, and fell in step beside Evren. Together, they navigated the late-afternoon traffic congesting the main avenue.

The Prime Bazaar rang with the cries of merchants trying to sell the last wares of the day to the pilgrims, treasure-hunters, and Vothmoti locals coming for the evening shopping. Ox-drawn wagons and rich carriages rumbled past, and pilgrims in their grey sackcloth surged in droves toward the Grand Chapel to watch the sunset through the stained glass window.

Evren paid little heed to the people around him. His mind mulled over Kaltris' offer, and he was so focused on his thoughts that he barely noticed the approaching guards. Only Daver's tug on his sleeve snapped him back to reality in time for him to catch sight of the Wardens heading right toward them. Evren's gut tightened as his eyes fell on the tall men with curved swords, white cloaks, and chain mail coats reinforced with round metal mirrors—protection from both physical and supernatural threats, the Wardens believed. He scrambled out of the street and ducked behind a cart just as the patrol marched past.

Heart hammering, he forced his mind to remain focused on getting out of sight safely. Relief filled him as he ducked into the alley that led between the Prime Bazaar and the Ward of Bliss. Before the sun had fully set, he and Daver reached the three-story building Swain and his crew called home.

"Well, look who returns!" Swain called out from his plush armchair. "Let's see your haul, then."

Evren hesitated. He'd worked all day for these coins, and he hated the idea of having to turn them over to Swain. Yet, it was the way things were done. He'd had to give Rhyris a share of anything he won in his fights in the temple, and it seemed he'd have to do the same with Swain.

"Twenty-two copper bits." He held out the coins. "Found a merchant willing to part with them." Swain didn't need to know *how* he'd gotten the money.

Swain's face registered amused surprise. "Not bad for a first day on the streets, newbie." He turned to Daver. "And what about you?"

"This is from *both* of us," Evren said, his voice firm.

47

"Izzat right?" Swain raised a dark eyebrow. "You ain't holding out on me, are you?"

"No." Evren shook his head. "Twenty-two copper bits between the two of us."

"Well then, tomorrow you'll just have to do better," Swain said as he plucked nine coins from Evren's hand.

"You said two out of every five," Evren growled. "Nine's more than your share."

"Consider it a peace offering." Swain's face went hard, and a dangerous light flashed in his eyes. "Do better tomorrow, or I'll take a larger share."

Evren wanted to retort, but the looming presence of four older, larger boys behind Swain stopped him. He could fight two or three, at most. Better to bide his time and bite his tongue.

"Got it." He choked the words out with effort then turned on his heel and stalked away.

"Until tomorrow, newbie!" Swain called after him.

Fury burned in Evren's chest as he stomped toward the spot Tomaz had set aside for him and Daver. He barely tasted his meager meal. The fire in his belly and the whirling thoughts in his head drowned out everything until darkness fell and he lay alone with anger and the dilemma.

What should he do? He'd fled the Lecterns and ended up with Swain, one torment replacing another. Kaltris had offered him a way out, but he couldn't abandon Daver.

Try as he might, he could find no solution to his problem.

Chapter Six

Evren's eyes drooped with fatigue, but his mind refused to let him rest. By the time the first light of dawn brightened the world around him, he hadn't slept a wink.

The sound of rustling blankets and thumping boots echoed around him, signaling the start of a new day for the street crew.

He rolled over and shook Daver's shoulder. "Get up, lazybones."

"Just a few more minutes," Daver protested and burrowed deeper into his ragged blanket.

"Come on. Kaltris will be expecting—"

"Newbie!" Swain's voice echoed through the Warren. "Get out here, newbie!"

Evren's gut tightened at the imperious tone in Swain's voice. Taking a deep breath, he climbed stiffly to his feet, already dressed, and pushed through the hanging canvas to the main area of the room.

Swain sat in his armchair throne, and his face broadened into a grin as Evren approached. "You're in luck. You're spending the day with me."

"Doing what?" Evren asked.

"Doing whatever the bloody hell I tell you to." Swain's eyes flashed. "You work for me, so you take my orders."

"Of course." Evren's mild tone concealed his anger. He'd learned to adopt the voice to placate Tinis before the Lectern compounded the punishment for some minor infraction of the temple's myriad rules.

"Good. Let's go." Swain turned on his heel and strode toward the door.

Evren cast a glance at the space he shared with Daver. He hated the idea of leaving the smaller boy alone, but Swain wouldn't take kindly to any hesitation or argument. He'd have to trust that Daver was smart enough to take care of himself.

In a way, he felt a bit of relief at being called away. He still hadn't come up with an answer for Kaltris, so he could use a few more hours to mull over the dilemma. Whatever Swain had in mind would serve as a welcome distraction.

He fell into step behind Swain. Three older, larger boys joined them, forming a protective group around Swain. Tomaz and another swarthy boy Evren hadn't seen the previous day rounded out their little procession as they wended through the muck-stained, refuse-clogged alleys of the Ward of Bliss.

Evren struggled to map the route through the maze but soon gave up trying. He knew they were headed northeast, in the general direction of the Master's Temple. As long as they didn't get too close, he had no reason to worry.

Swain paused in an alleyway that looked like all the others. "We're on enemy territory now, lads," he said in a low voice. "Mouth shut, eyes peeled. We're supposed to parley, but the Pincers are treacherous little pricks. Never know what they'll pull, so be ready for anything."

Evren had no idea who or what the Pincers were, but the wary look in the eyes of his companions made it clear that they were headed to a less-than-pleasant rendezvous.

Around the next corner, they came face to face with six youths as dirt-covered and rough-looking as Swain and his crew. A rival gang, perhaps?

"Well, well, if it isn't the Red Giggler and his fingernails!" called out the boy in the middle. Taller than the rest of his crew, he looked to be about fifteen or sixteen. A scar over his right eyebrow gave his handsome face a dangerous edge, and he alone wore clothes that seemed far too presentable for their dusty meeting place.

Swain snorted. "Be more creative with your insults, Hakim. Unless you're too stupid to think of anything better than mocking our names."

Hakim scowled. "Always the life of the party, Swain." His eyes roamed the rest of Swain's crew and stopped when they fell on Evren. "I see you've brought fresh meat to my grinder. Have we already beaten the rest of your boys bloody?" He cracked his knuckles loudly.

"Maybe," Swain said with a careless shrug. "I came to talk, but if we can't reach an agreement, I'm willing to settle things the street way."

"The only thing I'll agree to is keeping control of the Prime Bazaar." Hakim grinned. "So long as you keep your grubby Claws out of my prime spots, I won't have to turn any more of your boys into swine-food."

"You know the Prime Bazaar is our territory," Swain said with a shake of his head. "We've been running it since the Wardens swept up the last of the Crooked Hands two years ago. You Pincers took over the Court of Judgement, and the Talons have the kaffehouses."

Hakim shrugged. "Perhaps, but now we're looking to expand our operations. We're twice your size, which means we get twice the turf. The Prime Bazaar's just right for us. Unless you can stop us, we're taking it."

Swain cocked an eyebrow. "And leaving us with…?"

"Wherever the hell else you can scrape together a few coins." Hakim gave a dismissive wave. "I'm sure there are some pockets you can pick along Leper's Lane. Or maybe you can set up shop outside the North Gate and lighten the purses of the rich noblemen heading out to find the Lost City. If we haven't already lightened their purses for them, that is."

"Well, that just doesn't work for me," Swain said. "Prime Bazaar's ours and that's final."

"Then, I guess we're doing this the fun way." Hakim shrugged out of his bright red tunic and handed it to one of his companions. The boy had solid chest, shoulder, and midriff muscles, with nearly a dozen knife scars marring his deep gold skin. "You and me, boss against boss. Winner takes the turf. Or are you still refusing to face me yourself?"

Swain shot the boy a mocking grin. "You're not worth the effort." He turned and clapped Evren on the shoulder. "I'm willing to bet even the newbie can turn you inside out without breaking a sweat."

Hakim scowled. "Sending someone else to do your dirty work? They should call you the Yellow Belly, Swain."

Swain said nothing, but anger flashed in his eyes as he turned to Evren. "Tomaz told me how quickly you took him and his crew apart, which is the only reason I let you into the Claws. Time for you to prove him right."

Evren raised an eyebrow. "You're expecting me to fight him for you?"

"Not just fight," Swain growled. "Win. Prime Bazaar belongs to the Claws, and the only way the Pincers'll back off is if you pound their boss to a pulp. Lose the fight, we lose the turf. If that happens, I won't just make you pay." His expression turned hard, cruel. "Tomaz will suffer. And your little brother."

Evren went cold inside as he saw Tomaz' pale face. From the boy's expression, he had no doubt Swain would keep his word.

"I'll fight," he said, "but not for free."

Swain's eyes narrowed. "What?"

Evren fixed Swain with a hard glare. "I win this fight, you never touch Daver again. *Ever.*"

For a moment, Swain remained silent. "That's it?" he asked, snorting. "No better room, no higher status? No coins or clothes? That's all you want?"

"Yes." Evren nodded. "Those are my terms." The same terms he'd reached with Rhyris, Dracat, and all of the other ninth-years organizing the fights in the Master's Temple. His willingness to fight had kept Daver out of the ring. He'd fight again if it meant keeping Daver safe from Swain's ruthlessness.

"Done." Swain shook his head and threw up his hands. "And here I was expecting a big ask."

Evren sized up his opponent as he strode around Swain. Hakim was easily a hand and a half taller than him, his shoulders broader, his arms longer. The scars on his hands, forearms, and chest spoke of surviving numerous knife and fist-fights. He stood in the stance of an experienced fighter: feet spread slightly, right foot back, knees bent in a crouch, shoulders squared, chin tucked low. Despite his mocking smile, his eyes remained fixed on Evren and a hint of wary tension lined his face.

"You know the rules?" Hakim asked.

Evren shook his head.

"Last man standing's the victor." Hakim rolled his shoulders, cracking his neck loudly. "Try and give me a decent fight, eh? Make it a little fun at least."

Evren stopped just out of the boy's reach and squared off without a word. Loud mouths never won fights.

"You got this, Hakim!" cried one of the Pincers behind Evren's opponent.

"Take him down!" called Tomaz.

Evren turned to glance over his right shoulder and shoot a thumbs-up to his crew. He heard a sharp intake of Hakim's breath and the scrape of booted feet on the ground.

Just as he'd hoped, Hakim had taken the bait.

Instead of turning back—no doubt to meet the powerful punch aimed at his face or midsection—Evren continued spinning to the right, twisted his hips, and drove his right heel back in a mule kick. Hakim's punch slid over his dropping left shoulder, and his kick caught the Pincer's leader in the gut. The boy's breath exploded from his lungs and he staggered backward.

Evren regained his balance in an instant and pursued Hakim, throwing quick jabs to knock him off-guard and set up a powerful right cross that again struck the larger boy in the gut, right below the ribs. He ducked Hakim's wild swing, but the boy's spinning backfist caught him in the side of the face. The blow rocked him for an instant, and Hakim waded in with both fists. Evren had to give ground to avoid the powerful, uncontrolled punches.

Hakim's blows slowed as he tired quickly, and Evren seized the opportunity to bring his left fist up into Hakim's liver. The larger boy hunched over his right side, and Evren snapped off a low kick that caught Hakim in the left knee. Hakim's leg wobbled and he stumbled off-balance. Evren's body shot struck him in the gut a third time.

Vomit exploded from Hakim's mouth, spewing across the muddy alley. Hakim fell to his hands and knees, gasping and retching. Evren didn't give him a chance to recover but brought his knee around into the side of Hakim's head. The blow sent the larger boy to his face in the mud. Evren finished him off with a sharp kick to his face, and Hakim lay still, unconscious. Blood trickled from his broken nose and split lip to mingle with the vomit and muck covering the ground.

When Evren looked up, he found the five remaining Pincers staring at him and their fallen leader open-mouthed. For a moment, utter silence filled the alleyway.

"Hah!" Swain's laughter shattered the calm. "How do you like *that*, Hakim?"

Evren glanced back in time to see Swain walking the five steps to where the larger boy lay unconscious. He snorted loudly and spat a gob of phlegm onto Hakim's prone form.

"Champion!" Swain clapped Evren on the back. "Anyone else want to take a run at him?"

None of the Pincers seemed inclined to answer.

"Then, the outcome is final," Swain said in a cold voice. "Prime Bazaar is ours, and if I hear any of you pricks are angling or lifting on our turf, I'm going to send my champion here to hunt you down. Is that clear?"

"Y-Yes," stammered one of the Pincers.

"Good." Swain sneered. "Now, get your boss out of here before he drowns in his own vomit."

The five boys raced to gather up the unconscious Hakim and haul him back down the alley.

Swain remained unmoving, watching the retreating Pincers with a cold scowl. Once the boys had disappeared, he turned to Evren and wrapped a hand around his shoulder. "You did good, newbie. Where in the Keeper's name did you learn to fight like that?"

"Hell," Evren said in a low voice. He had more than fifty fights under his belt— both hard-won victories and bone-shattering defeats. Hakim hadn't come close to being his toughest battle.

Swain cocked an eyebrow. "Fine," he said. "You don't want to tell me, that's your right. But the fact remains that you fight like a bloody demon. You and me, we're going far together."

Evren shrugged out of Swain's grip. "Only if you hold up your end of our deal."

"Our deal?" Swain gave a dismissive wave. "Keeper's teeth, you keep dropping opponents like that, you can ask for whatever you want!" He clapped Evren's shoulder. "Starting with a drink of the finest wine you've ever tasted. On me!"

The mercurial shift in Swain's personality sent a shudder down Evren's spine. He'd fought opponents like Swain before, and they were dangerous in their unpredictability. He couldn't abandon Daver to go with Kaltris; now that Swain knew what he could do, there was no way the Claws' leader would let him leave. Deal or no, Daver would suffer if Evren fled.

Once again, he was trapped with no way out. He'd exchanged his prison at the Master's Temple for another on the streets.

Chapter Seven

Swain's offer of drinks had turned into a full-blown mid-morning meal in the quiet back room of The House of Wisdom, an inn famous for its stuffed grape leaves. In the comfort of the private dining chamber, Evren forgot all about his worries for a few minutes as he dug into the generously-spiced mixture of rice, meat, and vegetables swimming in rich ox-tail broth. He hadn't eaten a proper meal in days and had no idea when he'd get another. He'd enjoy Swain's generous mood while it lasted.

Yet, once he'd eaten his fill, he found himself worrying about Daver. As Swain kept ordering more goblets of the delicious Nyslian red wine, Evren couldn't stop wondering what the smaller apprentice was doing. Had he gone back to Kaltris to earn a few more coins, or was he waiting back at their Warren for him to return?

Thoughts of Kaltris soured Evren's mood. If the merchant couldn't take him and Daver both, he'd have to reject his kind offer. Even if Kaltris agreed to accept both of them, he wasn't certain he could leave the street gang anyway. Now that Swain knew what he could do, the Claws' leader would want to keep him close.

"Drink up, newbie!" Swain clapped him on the back and nudged his goblet closer. "It's a great day to be a Claw. We got our turf back from those Pincer pricks, and Hakim's going to think twice before trying to take it from us again. Hell, *all* the other gangs are going to."

The Claw leader leaned forward and dropped his voice. "You didn't just beat Hakim. You destroyed him. I wouldn't be surprised if the Pincers have a new leader before nightfall."

Evren hid a wince. Back in the alley, his survival instincts had kicked in and he'd fought for his life. He hadn't meant to trounce Hakim, but he'd faced so many larger, stronger, and heavier opponents in the Master's Temple that he'd battled the Pincer leader the way he'd planned to fight Engerack. Dracat, Rhyris, and the other ninth-years always stopped the fight before one of the fighters ended up dead, but they always let it continue until one of them was beaten bloody and senseless.

But that was the way of life, wasn't it? No one else would fight for him. No one would protect him from people like Swain or the Lecterns.

Swain's face grew suddenly serious. "But we're not just here to celebrate." He glanced toward the closed door that shut their tastefully-decorated back room off from The House of Wisdom's common room. "We're here to talk, you and me."

"About?" Evren raised an eyebrow.

"About the Lecterns." Swain drew something from within his robes and placed it on the table.

Ice slithered down Evren's spine as his gaze rested on the platinum crescent moon pendant Swain had taken from him. He tried to conceal his anxiety with a nonchalant question. "What about them?"

Swain scratched his chin. "Well, about why exactly you and your brother have their pendants." He held up a hand before Evren could respond. "Don't bother trying to deny it. I went to a friend of mine to see about melting it down, and when he refused to so much as touch it, I found myself growing curious. Imagine my surprise when I hear the tale of two apprentices fleeing the Master's Temple two nights ago. Then I think to myself, 'I know two lads who might just fit the bill'."

"Do you really believe that Daver and I—" Evren began.

"Damn right I do!" Swain's quiet tone held a dangerous, menacing edge. "This pendant is all the proof I need. That, and the fact that you two show up on my turf the morning after two apprentices around your age escape the Lecterns."

Evren's gut clenched. He studied Swain's face for any indication of what he'd say next. He had no doubt the Claws' leader would hand him over to the Lecterns if it got him what he wanted. The question now was what the bloody hell did Swain want?

"Rest easy, newbie." Swain gave him a hollow smile. "I'm not going to turn you in."

Something about the way he said it made Evren uneasy.

"See, when I hear about two apprentices escaping the temple, it gets me thinking." Swain tapped a filthy fingernail against his now-empty goblet, filling the small room with a repetitive *clinking*. "If apprentices can get out, maybe it means there's a way for someone to get *in*."

Evren's stomach tightened, and the wine threatened to come back up. Swain couldn't be so foolish as to think—

The Red Grinner grinned. "You and me, we're going to rob the Master's Temple."

"Not a bloody chance!" Evren clenched his fists. "There's no way I'm going back in there and much less to steal from the Lecterns."

Swain's smile froze, and his eyes turned icy. "Did I make it sound like I was asking?" He leaned forward. "I'm *telling* you we're doing it."

"And I'm telling you trying to get into the Master's Temple is the stupidest, most suicidal thing you could do," Evren retorted. "Between the Wardens guarding the front and all the apprentices and Lecterns inside, there's no way we can get in and out unnoticed."

"You and your brother managed just fine."

"We got lucky!" Evren slammed his palm onto the table. "We escaped because all of the Lecterns were trying to get a look at the Caliph during the midnight service. It was only by the Mistress' luck that all the apprentices were locked away in their cells. There's no way we'll get lucky twice."

"Sure there is." A smug grin spread Swain's face. "You'll find a way, because if you don't, I'm going to beat your brother to death right in front of you." His hand dropped to his dagger. "After that, I'll cut off your hands and feet, then move on to your tiny prick and shove it down your throat. Imagine a death like that, choking on your own manhood."

Across the table, Tomaz' face had gone pale. Even two of the larger boys who served as Swain's bodyguards seemed stunned by the threat. Only the third, the largest of the lot, showed no surprise. His hand also hovered by the rusted knife at his belt, and he watched Evren with wary eyes.

For a moment, Evren contemplated drawing his own blade and trying to kill Swain. He'd never taken a life before, but he'd come mighty close during his fights in the temple. To save Daver's life, he'd seriously consider it.

"I'll give you a chance to think about it." Swain's congenial smile returned. "Let's say, sunset tonight? If I haven't gotten an answer, I'll have Herond here bring Daver to me then I'll send every other Claw to bring you in. You fight well, but you'll be just one against the rest of us." He said all this without losing his broad grin. "And, for every bruise you inflict, I'll give Daver two. For every cut or bloody nose, I'll double it on your brother. Is that clear?"

A fist of iron squeezed Evren's heart, and acid surged in the back of his throat.

"You're welcome to try and run," Swain said, taking a sip of his wine. "The desert sands are always thirsty for more corpses. But know that I've got people keeping an eye on your brother right now. If you do try to flee, I'll know, and I'll send the Lecterns after you. You won't get far." He set the goblet down on the table and held up the pendant before Evren's eyes. "Trust me when I say it's in your best interest to give me what I want."

The Claws' leader slung the pendant around his neck, pushed back his chair, and strode from the back room with his three bodyguards in tow. Tomaz hesitated only long enough to shoot a remorseful gaze at Evren before he followed.

Evren sat in stunned silence. His stomach churned in time with his racing thoughts. What could he do? He had no doubt Swain would follow through on his threat. His only hope lay in finding Daver, losing the boys following the apprentice, and convincing Kaltris to take them both with him. They could hide among the crates piled on the merchant's wagon until they had left Vothmot far behind. He had no idea what Mountainfall had to offer, but he ought to be able to find some way to earn coins there. They could start a new life away from Vothmot, the Master's Temple, and Swain.

He had to find Daver. Now.

The thought snapped him into action. He knocked over his chair in his hurry to race out of the back room and stumbled into a wobbling drunk, sending the man crashing into a wooden table. Angry shouts of protest followed him out into the street.

The food and wine sloshed in his belly as he ran, but he swallowed the surge of vomit before it came up. The Summer Market was only ten or fifteen streets away. He'd start the search for Daver there. If the apprentice wasn't with Kaltris or begging on the same corner, he'd head back to the Warren and see what he could find. Someone had to know where Daver was—someone who wasn't working for Swain.

He slowed to a walk as he caught sight of a patrol of Wardens. Sunlight glinted off their mirrored plate armor and the naked scimitars in their hands. Evren ducked out of the street before they caught sight of him and cut through an alleyway that led toward the marketplace.

A sense of urgency pounded in the back of his mind. He glanced up at the sky and found the sun just passing midday. He had until sundown to find Daver and escape Swain. Would he have enough time?

His lungs burned and his legs ached as he slipped back onto the main avenue and raced toward the Summer Market. He scanned the rows of stalls in search of the one where he'd find Kaltris. To his dismay, the stall was empty.

"Where's Kaltris?" he asked Jodech, a tall merchant who wore his dark hair in a single braid that hung down to his waist.

"Gone," came the terse reply from Kaltris' neighbor.

Evren chafed with impatience as Jodech returned his attention to the elderly, well-dressed woman. He raced up the street but saw no sign of Daver. By the time he ran back, Jodech had finished with his customer.

"Where did he go?" Evren demanded.

61

"How should I know?" Jodech threw up his hands in exasperation.

"He askin' about Kaltris?" The question came from Cheeril, the onion seller with a stall beyond Jodech's.

"Yes!" Evren dashed toward the red-haired woman. "Do you know where he is?"

"Aye." Cheeril spoke in a strange accent foreign to Vothmot, and she had skin far paler than his own deep brown. "Stopped by this mornin' to bring me these." She gestured to a pile of garlic bulbs. "Said he couldn't sell them and didn't want them to end up rottin'. When I asked why, he said somethin' about a last-moment trip to Brittlewall to fetch an urgent load."

Brittlewall was a village half a day's fast ride to the east. At the pace of Kaltris' mule-drawn carriage, the merchant would be gone until noon the following day.

Evren's heart sank, and the strength seemed to leave his body. He couldn't brave the desert on his own, not without a horse and supplies. Fifteen copper bits and a silver half-drake would be nowhere near enough to get him out of Vothmot before sunset. He had to come up with another plan, but first he had to find Daver.

"Thank you." He nodded to Jodech and Cheeril.

"You lookin' fer work today?" Jodech asked. "I can pay you ten copper bits for—"

"Sorry," Evren said. "I've got something important I need to do."

"Might it have somethin' to do with yer brother and the Wardens?" Cheeril asked, her pale brow furrowed.

Evren froze. "Wardens?"

"Aye." Cheeril bobbed her head, setting her long red braids flying. "Saw 'em marchin' in his direction not half an hour past, and when I turned back, they was haulin' him away." She dropped her voice to a whisper. "Ye in trouble with the Wardens, lad?"

Evren's mouth went bone dry. Fear thrummed deep within him. The Wardens had Daver, which meant they'd taken him back to the Master's Temple.

There was only one thing to do.

Without a word to either of the two merchants, he raced up the street toward the Prime Bazaar, then ducked into the adjoining alley. His heart hammered against his ribs as he sprinted through the muck-covered lanes, bounced off a stone wall, and thundered up the steps into the three-story building the Claws called home.

Swain seemed surprised to see him. "Good to see you've made—"

"I'll do it." Evren cut him off with a snarl. "I'll get you into the Master's Temple and help you steal whatever the bloody hell you want."

"Had a change of heart, have we?" Swain raised an eyebrow.

"They have Daver," Evren snapped. "But you knew that, didn't you?"

"Sure." Swain nodded. "Just heard the news the moment I arrived."

"Then, we're going in. Tonight." A hard knot of determination formed in Evren's stomach. "But only if you swear you'll help me get Daver out."

"I swear," Swain said without hesitation.

"No, not like that." Evren drew his knife and stepped forward.

Swain's bodyguards tensed, but the Red Grinner only raised an eyebrow.

Evren made no move to attack. "You've already proven how much your word means. Swear a blood oath, on all the gods of Einan. An oath not even you will break easily."

Swain's eyes narrowed. "You ask a high price, newbie."

"And offer a high reward in return," Evren snarled. "You want the treasure of the Master's Temple, you swear the oath."

Swain studied him for a moment, then nodded. "So be it." He took Evren's dagger and sliced his palm. Raising his hand, he let blood drip onto the stone floor as he spoke. "On all the gods of Einan, I swear that I will help you get your brother out if you show me how to get into the Master's Temple. If I break this oath, may my soul suffer in the darkest hells for all eternity." He handed the dagger, still stained crimson with his blood, back to Evren. "Satisfied?"

"Yes." Evren sheathed the blade. "Now, if we want to get into the Master's Temple, here's what we're going to need…"

Chapter Eight

The darkness of the night did little to dispel the nervous tension writhing in Evren's gut. The cloud cover provided shadows to conceal him and the others as they snuck through the alleys toward the rear of the Master's Temple, but he couldn't shake the feeling of dread that had settled over him. The stink of the rotting corpse against the wall, still undiscovered by the Wardens, twisted his stomach.

Too much could go wrong. Even if the older apprentices hadn't told the Lecterns of their back way out, there was always a chance the Wardens would post men to watch the rear of the temple. Someone could be in the Gardens of Prudence despite the late hour, or an apprentice could be awake as he crept into the cells. Then there was the matter of Swain. Evren didn't fully trust the Claws' leader, even with that binding oath he'd sworn.

A hint of his anxiety faded as he found only empty darkness and silence in the alleyway that ran along the temple's outer wall. The rope ladder he'd used to escape hadn't been moved, which meant the Wardens and Lecterns hadn't thought to search the rear of the temple. If his luck held, he could get in and out without being discovered. Once this was done, he'd never have to return to the Master's Temple again. Swain would have his big score and might relax his vigilance long enough for Evren and Daver to flee with Kaltris. He could leave Vothmot and his old life behind.

He stopped at the rope ladder and waited for Swain, Tomaz, and Rosser, one of Swain's bodyguards, to catch up.

"Got that second rope ladder?" he asked.

Rosser, a large, curly-haired lad with equal parts muscle and fat, removed a satchel from his shoulder and pulled out the coils of rope. Rags wrapped the metal hooks at the end of the ladder, the perfect padding to muffle the sound of steel on stone.

"Once we're up, we leave one rope ladder hanging down the outside of the wall so we can make a quick getaway," he told the others.

Swain turned to Rosser. "You're with the newbie. Stick with him and help him get his brother out. As for you, Tomaz, you're with me."

"You remember where to find the valuables?" Evren asked.

"Of course," Swain snapped. "Fifth floor of the temple proper, the High Lecterns' level."

"Good." Evren nodded. "The valuables in the Grand Chapel and the Master's Nave are worth more, but there's a higher chance of you being spotted. But there's more than enough in the halls outside the High Lecterns' chambers to make it worth your while." Between the Fehlan ice candles, brass candlesticks, and gold and silver statuettes, Swain ought to come away with more than enough loot.

"There better be." Swain's eyes shot Rosser a meaningful look. The bigger boy wasn't there to *help* Evren so much as make sure he didn't try to run off.

He shot a glance up at the sky. The thick cloud cover offered more than enough darkness, but he'd waited until well past midnight to be certain the Master's Temple would be as empty and silent as possible.

"The apprentices will be awakened in a few hours for morning lessons, so we've got to move while they're all still asleep in their cells."

Swain thrust a chin toward the ladders. "After you, newbie." He lowered his voice to a menacing whisper. "Anything goes wrong, I'll hunt you down and cut you to pieces. Clear?"

Evren responded with a grunt. He'd expect no less from the Claws' leader. He clambered up the rope ladder he'd left hanging in his escape while Swain scaled the one they'd brought for the break-in. He peered cautiously over the wall and scanned the Gardens of Prudence for any movement. Only the merry bubbling of the fountains reached his ears, and the flickering light of the oil lanterns revealed an empty garden.

He gave Swain a thumbs-up and pulled himself onto the top of the wall. Swain helped him haul up one of the rope ladders and hook it onto the inside of the wall. Evren shimmied down first, followed by Swain a minute later.

Evren's heart hammered as he turned away from the wall and crept through the shadows toward the hedges. Most of the Lecterns would be abed at this time of night, but some of the older priests tended to take late-night walks to combat their insomnia. And, if Rhyris and Dracat had a fight on for tonight, there could be apprentices and priests both slinking around the temple.

He had to hope his luck held. Daver was counting on him.

The hedges rustled as Swain, Tomaz, and Rosser crouched beside him. "Anything?" Swain asked.

"No signs of life yet." Evren's gut clenched. "But that doesn't mean there aren't Lecterns or apprentices roaming around inside. We've got to make this quick."

"Ten minutes." Tomaz nodded. He patted the empty sack hanging from his shoulder. "Get what we came for and get the hell out."

"This isn't our first job, you know." Swain's voice was tight, curt. "*You're* the newbie here."

"I'm also the only one who knows his way around," Evren retorted. "Just stick to the route I drew out for you, and you'll get in and out unseen."

They'd spent the afternoon and evening planning the heist, and he'd drawn a crude map from his memories of the temple's interior. He'd never be an architect, but it would guide the others to where they needed to go.

He drew in a deep breath. "Go!"

Slipping free of the hedge, he pounded past the raised stone pool, across the pristine laws, and up the marble stone walkway toward the shadows of the rear entrance. His gut clenched as he slithered into the tunnel, but he found only an empty temple ahead. He skirted the pillared main nave and slipped in silence toward the hallway that led toward White Tower.

Swain and Tomaz turned onto the ascending staircase to the temple's upper floors, leaving Evren alone with Rosser. He was keenly aware of the larger boy's presence at his back, the sound of his loud breathing. Doubtless Swain had given Rosser instructions of what to do if he tried to pull anything. So be it. He had no reason to deviate from the plan until *after* he'd freed Daver. Swain would get what he wanted, and Evren would get his friend.

His breath caught in his lungs as a sleepy, white-haired priest—he recognized the ebony cane and wispy white hair of Lectern Estland—hobbled out of a meditation chamber and into the hall. Evren hauled Rosser down a side passage that led to White Tower, albeit in a more circuitous route.

To his relief, they encountered no more Lecterns or apprentices as they slipped down the lamp-lit corridors, and his heart leapt as he reached the entrance to White Tower. Down the stairs he went, then he turned into the plain stone hallway that would take him to the apprentices' cells and Daver.

He slowed and clung to the wall as he slipped toward his cell, pulse pounding in his ears. The chambers nearest the entrance belonged to the older apprentices. His and Daver's cell was the tenth door down. He couldn't risk anyone waking up as he tried to free his friend.

Rosser's breathing sounded terribly loud in the silence, and the boy's thick, too-large boots made far more noise than Evren would have liked. After just three steps, he'd had enough.

He whirled to Rosser and pressed a hand against the larger boy's chest. "Stay!" he mouthed and pointed down to the bigger boy's feet. "Too loud. Keep watch."

Rosser tensed but nodded. "Go," he muttered.

Heart hammering, Evren glided in silence toward his cell. His mouth grew dry as he passed three cells, four, then five. It took all his self-control to keep his breathing steady and quiet, to maintain a slow pace when he wanted to break into a run. Every minute spent in the temple increased the chance he'd be caught.

He froze as he heard voices from within the eighth cell down, and his hand dropped to the dagger at his belt. He had no desire to use it, but he wouldn't let anyone stop him from freeing Daver.

The tension drained from his shoulder as he recognized the voice. Garnet, a fifth-year apprentice, had a tendency to walk and talk in his sleep. The sleeping boy rattled off a stream of loud gibberish for a long moment before the cell fell silent again.

Evren blew out a silent breath and continued creeping toward the tenth cell. He froze as he saw the new addition to his cell door: a padlock securing the deadbolt. The Lecterns had locked Daver inside his cell—so which Lectern had the key?

He shot a glance back at Rosser. If the older boy was a thief, perhaps he knew how to pick locks. Rhyris had boasted about the skill he'd picked up from studying one of the many books in the Vault of Stars, but Evren had never seen it done.

But Rosser made far too much noise, which raised the chance one of the sleeping apprentices would be awakened. No, he had to find another way.

An idea popped into his mind. He drew his dagger and shoved the blade between the two shanks of the padlock. The steel was strong, but would it be stronger than the iron padlock? He gave a few experimental twists, but the dagger's blade bent from the strain.

He hesitated, uncertain if he should continue trying. The crude kitchen knife was his only weapon, and he'd need it if Swain tried to come after him and Daver, or if he had to fight his way out of the temple. Yet, he'd come all this way to free Daver. He could find, buy, or steal another blade.

He twisted the padlock, tightened his grip on the dagger's handle, and gave a short, sharp tug on the knife. Two loud *snaps* echoed in the corridor in quick succession, followed by the *clunk* of the lock and the tinkling of the steel blade hitting the stone floor. Evren's gut tightened as he stared at the shattered knife, but he pushed aside the momentary worry and reached for the deadbolt. He winced at the groaning of the door's hinges as he pushed it open and slithered inside the cell.

"Daver?" he hissed into the dense blackness. "You in here?"

"Oh, he's in here." The cold voice sent a shiver of fear down Evren's spine.

A firestriker sparked in the darkness, and a tiny tongue of fire illuminated Rhyris' angular face.

"Welcome back, Evren," the older boy said with a cruel grin. "Good to see you haven't forgotten your old pals."

The ninth-year touched the firestriker to the wick of a candle, and the faint light shone on the four figures in the cell.

Evren's gut clenched as he caught sight of Daver's prone form. The smaller boy lay curled in a heap, blood trickling from wounds on his face, his back a mess of red stripes from Lectern Uman's cane. Filthy rags held him bound and gagged, and fear filled his eyes as he stared up at Evren.

Rhyris and Dracat stood above Daver, a wicked light gleaming in their eyes. Dracat lit a second candle from Rhyris' and turned to Evren with a vicious smile. "You skipped out on your fight two nights ago. It's only fair you make up for it now."

Ice ran down Evren's spine as he turned to the last figure in the room. Engerack, a seventh-year apprentice, stood taller than even Rosser, his huge body made of solid muscle. He flexed fists the size of Lectern Nallin's famous Wintertide ham hocks and rolled his huge neck with a loud *crack*.

A smile spread Engerack's heavy features. "Looks like we're getting that fight after all."

Chapter Nine

Evren looked from Daver to Engerack to Rhyris and Dracat. "No." He shook his head. "I'm not going to fight."

"No?" Rhyris cocked an eyebrow. "You make it sound like you have a choice."

"The minute we heard your little weakling friend here was caught, we knew you'd be back for him," Dracat sneered. "We've had eyes watching the back wall ever since, just so we could be ready." He shook his head. "I didn't think you'd be foolish enough to come back tonight, but Rhyris was certain."

The sound of twenty cell doors opening echoed in the corridor behind Evren, accompanied by the stampede of slapping feet. He glanced back and found dozens of apprentices—many from Grey and Black Towers as well—crowding around the door. Eagerness shone in their eyes as they watched the confrontation.

Rhyris folded his arms. "Your choice is simple: fight or watch Engerack here shatter every bone in your little friend's body." He gestured down at Daver. "We won't kill him, though. He'll live the rest of his life a cripple, and it'll all be on your head."

"Those are my options?" Evren cocked his head. "Seems like I lose either way. Even if I fight, I still end up locked away in here." He pressed the stump of his shattered knife to his own throat. "I'd rather die than stay in the temple one more hour."

Rhyris and Dracat's eyebrows rose in surprise. Engerack seemed confused by this development. The seventh-year had the strength of an ox and the wits to match. Too many knocks to his head had dulled his mental edge.

Evren fixed the two ninth-year apprentices with a hard glare. "There's only one thing I'll fight for: freedom. For Daver *and* me. I win, we walk out of here."

"And if Engerack wins," Dracat snarled, "the Lecterns find *two* corpses in this cell tomorrow."

Evren's gut clenched. "So be it." He had no other choice, no better outcome. Survival and freedom were worth wagering his life. "Where are we fighting?"

Rhyris swept an expansive gesture at the bare stone walls of the cell. "Right here, of course!" A broad grin stretched his face. "No sense dragging it out or hauling you through the temple to the usual storage chamber. Less chance of the Lecterns catching us in here."

Evren drew in a deep breath, then nodded. "Fair enough." He turned his back on Engerack, removed his tunic, and folded it neatly. He handed the shirt and his shattered knife to Gadid, a sixth-year Crystal Tower apprentice standing beside the door. "I'll be expecting that back in a minute."

He spoke in a confident tone, but anxiety simmered within him. His stomach twisted in knots as he turned to face Engerack. The larger boy had squared off, his massive fists raised, a smile of anticipation twisting his lips. Evren could see it in Engerack's eyes: the bigger boy was ready to rip him apart.

Engerack was taller, heavier, stronger, and had longer arms than him. The seventh-year apprentice had more fights under his belt, better technique, and a high tolerance to pain. All Evren had was a will to live. If he lost, he died, and Daver with him.

He had one more advantage: he knew every detail of the cell. Four long steps wide and five steps long. Smaller, now that Rhyris, Daver, and Dracat occupied the far corner of the tiny room. He knew each stone, crack, and indentation in the floor, every irregularity in the walls. He'd paced this cell a thousand times, and his feet slid across the uneven stones with easy familiarity.

Engerack took one quick shuffling step forward and jabbed his massive right fist at Evren's face. Evren slipped the punch—Engerack started every fight the same way—then threw a sharp punch at the bigger boy's stomach. The apprentice didn't bother to block the blow. Evren winced at the pain in his knuckles; it felt like he'd struck the stone walls.

The flickering light of the candle made it hard to see, and he barely caught sight of Engerack's follow-up punch in time to duck. Right into Engerack's rising knee. The impact snapped his head up and back, and he stumbled backward to crash into the stone walls.

A single cheering shout rang out in the cell, but Rhyris' angry hiss turned the cries of the onlookers to low whispers. This far below ground, there was little chance the Lecterns would overhear, but the ninth-years weren't going to take any chances.

Evren pushed off the wall and shook his head to clear it. When he wiped his face, his hand came away bloody. Engerack's knee had re-opened his split lip.

The larger boy's eyes had gone flat, all expression drained from his face. The seventh-year might struggle with reading, writing, and sums, but when it came to fighting, he was as close to a savant as Evren had ever seen. His size gave him an advantage over every opponent—all but the near-insane Oldsek—and his understanding of bare-handed fighting techniques made him deadly.

Evren squared off, chin tucked close to his shoulder, balance spread between his left and right feet. He couldn't charge Engerack—it would have as much effect as a lamb charging a rabid wolf—so he had to find another way to get through his opponent's guard. The seventh-year was slower than him, barely. If he could slip past the bone-shattering punches, he might have a chance of laying Engerack out.

He ducked right, then left as Engerack jabbed at his face, then he slithered out of the way of a body shot. His answering punch to Engerack's liver struck hard muscle as the boy twisted his torso. Evren had to throw himself backward to avoid the powerful right cross aimed at his nose. He crashed against the wall again, but this time Engerack didn't pause to let him recover. The boy crossed the distance in one long step and laid into him with vicious body blows and hooks.

Evren desperately tried to protect his face and ribs, but Engerack was too experienced to be predictable. He punched high and low without discernible pattern, sending pain shivering through Evren's sides as his massive fists struck bone. Evren brought his knee up into the larger boy's groin, but Engerack caught it on his thigh. The impact knocked him backward a single pace, long enough for Evren to lift his foot, step on a stone protruding from the wall at his knee level, and leap at the boy. His flying punch cracked into Engerack's jaw with bruising force.

The seventh-year actually staggered back a second step, and Evren followed up with a low kick that snapped into Engerack's knee. The boy wobbled for a heartbeat, giving Evren a chance to bring his knee up into the underside of Engerack's chin. The big apprentice's head snapped backward and he fell onto his back.

A gasp of surprise echoed in the cell as all eyes watched Engerack's fall. But before Evren could draw in a single breath, Engerack rolled to his feet and charged with a furious roar. Massive arms wrapped around Evren's waist, lifted him from the ground, and slammed him into the wall.

Evren's head and back struck stone with jarring force. The world spun crazily around him as he slumped atop the messy pile of straw that had served as his bed. A moment later, pain blossomed in his ribs, his face, and his ribs again. Engerack's fourth kick knocked the breath from his lungs.

By instinct or sheer luck, he managed to roll out of the way of Engerack's next kick and came to his feet. Every part of him ached, and he gasped for air. His mind raced as he tried to decide his next move. Trading blows with Engerack wouldn't end well. No matter how much punishment he could take, Engerack could dish out more. His eyes went to the bloodied Daver huddling at Rhyris' feet. If he didn't fight smart, he'd never get out of this match alive.

Engerack stalked toward him, but Evren didn't wait for the bigger boy to close the distance. He charged, feigning an intent to wrap his arms around Engerack's waist. When the seventh-year planted his feet to absorb the impact, Evren slowed his rush and snapped a kick up into the boy's chin. Engerack staggered backward, and his heels caught on an uneven section of floor. Evren leapt high into the air and drove both feet into Engerack's chest. The bigger boy toppled backward, arms flailing, and struck the ground with a loud *thump*.

Evren landed hard as well, a twinge of pain running down his right arm and already-tender ribs. But he bounced up to his feet and threw himself onto the prone Engerack. The bigger boy was too dazed by the fall to even raise his hands and defend himself as Evren rained blow after blow onto his face. Crimson spurted from the boy's broken nose and split lips. Shattered teeth sliced into Evren's knuckles, adding more of Evren's blood into the mix. He didn't stop punching but kept whaling on the downed Engerack. If he stopped, if he let up, Engerack could recover enough to win the fight—and Daver would die.

"Enough!" Two sets of hands seized his pumping arms and dragged him off Engerack. "The fight's over!"

When the haze of pain and fury cleared, Evren found Engerack lying still. His chest rose and fell, but his eyes had rolled back into his head. Adrenaline coursed through his veins, and his hands trembled with the desire to keep hitting something, anything. Pent-up rage over his treatment by the Lecterns, his fellow apprentices, and Swain burned like a wildfire within him. He tore free of the restraining hands and whirled on Dracat and Rhyris. He ached to give them both a taste of the torment they'd inflicted upon him and the other apprentices.

"It's over!" Dracat shouted, raising his hands like a shield. Fear flashed in the ninth-year's eyes. He had just watched his champion get beaten into submission, and nothing but empty air stood between him and the furious victor.

"Evren, you won." Rhyris actually took a half-step backward, bumping into the wall. "Take him and go!"

The sight of Daver's bloodied back and filthy bonds only added to Evren's fury. He tore them off Daver's arms and pulled the gag gently from his mouth. He wasn't strong enough to carry Daver, so he helped the younger boy stand on wobbling legs.

He turned to the two ninth-years with a hard glare. "Pray to the Master that the Lecterns never find me." He thrust a finger at Engerack's prone form. "I'll do worse than that if I ever see you again."

Silence met his proclamation as he helped Daver limp from the cell. He paused only long enough to reclaim his tunic and shattered knife, then pushed his way through the apprentices gathered in the hallway and left the cells far behind for the last time.

Chapter Ten

Rosser's eyes were wide as he fell in step beside Evren. He'd managed to get a decent view of the end of the fight, and he gave Evren a wide berth. He actually flinched when Evren snapped, "Help me carry him!" and leapt to heed the command with alacrity.

Evren helped Daver limp up the stairs and through the temple proper, but the smaller boy was almost too weak to walk on his own. Were it not for Rosser's strong arms, they might not have made it. As it was, they had to half-carry, half-drag the sagging apprentice down the corridors.

He scanned every hall they passed, both for Lecterns and for Tomaz or Swain. He saw no sign of the Claws, but right now his only concern was getting Daver out before they were discovered. Gritting his teeth, he tried to ignore the pain in his ribs, head, and face as he supported the stumbling apprentice. Thankfully, Rosser carried a lot of Daver's weight, so they made quick progress through the corridors.

Evren breathed a sigh of relief as he turned into the corridor that led out into the Gardens of Prudence. The way was clear, no Lecterns or Wardens between him and the dark night. He hustled Daver down the passage as fast as he could manage. Getting Daver over the wall would prove challenging—hell, he wasn't sure *he* could get over in his battered state—but one problem at a time.

He took a single step into the garden when a sound froze him in place. His gut clenched as he saw a tall, thick-shouldered figure lounging in the shallow pool at the northeastern corner of the gardens. It could only be one person: Lectern Uman. The cool water soothed the pain in the Lectern's injured knee, and he alone bathed at this time of night.

"Stop!" he hissed at Rosser. The bigger boy complied, his eyes darting to the Lectern.

Evren's mind raced. If Uman saw him fleeing, he'd raise the alarm. Even though it would take the Lectern time to hobble back to the temple, it would be less than five minutes before the priests and Wardens flooded the streets and alleys around the Court of Judgement to hunt them down. He and the drooping Daver wouldn't get far enough away.

His hand went to the broken dagger bundled in his clothing, but he couldn't bring himself to draw it. He was a fighter but not a murderer. He couldn't kill a man in cold blood. Not even after what Lectern Uman had done to him time and again.

The Lectern had his back turned to them, and he reclined against the edge of the pool, visibly relaxed. If they kept quiet as they hurried, they could get across the gardens and into the hedges without alerting Uman. They might have to wait until the Lectern finished bathing before they scaled the rope ladder, but at least they'd get away unnoticed.

He pressed a finger to his lips, then pointed to Daver and mimed carrying him like a sack of potatoes. Rosser nodded and lifted the smaller apprentice onto his shoulders. Evren froze at Daver's groan, but the boy bit on his lip to stifle more cries.

Heart hammering, Evren motioned for Rosser to go ahead. He'd keep an eye on Uman and be ready to act if the Lectern caught them—though, what that action would be, he had no idea. Better to remain quiet and get out of sight unseen.

Rosser's heavy breathing sounded terribly loud in Evren's ears, but he forced himself to keep padding along behind the larger boy. His heart skipped a beat as they crept onto the tiled walkway that skirted the pool and led toward the hedges. This was the critical moment. Either they passed unnoticed or Lectern Uman heard them and—

"Who goes there?" The Lectern's rumbling voice sent a shiver down Evren's spine. Water splashed as the priest sat up and turned toward them.

He shoved Rosser hard toward the hedges, then leapt backward into Lectern Uman's field of vision. He had to keep the priest's attention fixed on him long enough for Rosser to get out of sight with Daver. Then what? He had no idea, but he knew he had to ensure Daver reached safety before he worried about himself.

"Evren!" Lectern Uman hissed. The light of the flickering torches cast eerie shadows on his face as he fixed Evren with a stern glare. "You have returned to us."

Evren's gut tightened. Even now, he felt his mind retreating as it always did when the Lectern came to him for "prayers". The cold numbness seeped over him and his muscles turned to stone. He stood in the open, yet he felt as trapped and helpless as he had when locked in his cell waiting for his punishment.

Lectern Uman stood up from the shallow pool, water dripping from his naked body, down his twisted hip and knee. "I am glad to see you have repented of your folly." He took a limping step toward Evren, arms outstretched. "While you must face the consequences of your choices, the Master is a god of mercy. He will accept you back into the temple with open arms, as will we all. First repentance, then forgivene—"

"No." The word burst from Evren's lips. "No," he repeated, a fire burning in his chest. "I will not face your consequences, nor will I submit to your abuse any longer."

Instead of fleeing, he found himself taking a step closer to the Lectern. "For years, I have been slave to this temple, too afraid to act for myself. No more!"

His voice rose to a shout, and he made no attempt to silence his fury. He stood alone in the garden with the man who had tormented him for years. He would hold his tongue no longer.

"I am free of you!" Venom dripped from his words. "I am free of your punishments, your rules, your temple. I will not return. You cannot make me."

"Come now, Evren," Lectern Uman said in a soothing tone. He reached for the cane leaning against the raised stone wall surrounding the pool and leaned his weight on it. "You are young, and the ways of the Master are still far above your understand—"

"No!" Evren shouted. "You claim to be a servant of the god of virtue and nobility, but there is nothing virtuous about *any* of you! Nothing in this place has anything noble. Not the beatings, the fights, the starvations, and the abuse. This is vile, the work of Kharna himself, not the Master."

"Still your tongue!" Lectern Uman snapped. In a moment, his expression transformed from placating to cruel, edged with cold fury. "Your words reveal the wickedness within you. I can see that it will take more than a few hours of hunger and thirst to cleanse the evil in your heart. But it will be done, by the Master's grace. I will make certain of it personally."

The Lectern took a shuffling step toward Evren, and the weighted end of his cane whipped toward Evren's head. Instinct kicked in, and Evren ducked, shuffled forward, and lashed out. His punch, driven by all the force of his fury and bitterness, collided with the Lectern's jaw. The blow snapped the man's head to one side hard enough to daze him. The Lectern stumbled backward, and his good foot caught on the edge of an uneven tile. He stepped onto his twisted leg, which crumbled beneath his weight, and crashed onto his back. His head struck the inner edge of the raised stone wall surrounding the pool and a loud *crack* echoed in the darkened garden.

Lectern Uman's wide eyes stared at Evren in horror, but life slowly faded as blood gushed from his shattered skull.

A shiver of horror coursed through Evren as he watched the halo of crimson spreading in the water of the pool. He'd beaten many opponents into unconsciousness, but he'd never killed anyone.

The urge to vomit gripped him, yet a mingled sense of triumph and relief drove it away. He was free. Lectern Uman would never touch him—or any other apprentices—again. He hadn't intended to kill the man, but Einan was better off for it.

"I am your victim no longer!" Evren snarled.

With one last glance at his tormentor, Evren turned and raced toward the hedges. In the dark shadows of the wall, he found Rosser trying in vain to help a wobbling Daver stand and climb the rope ladder.

"Daver!" Evren called. "You need to do it yourself. You need to climb so we can get out of here."

"Evren?" Daver seemed disoriented, weak from blood loss and the beating he'd received. "What are you doing?"

"I came back for you," Evren said, taking his friend's hand. "We're getting out of here."

"What happened to you?" Daver asked, squinting at Evren's face. "You're all bloody."

"I'll tell you about it later. For now, you have to be strong. You have to climb."

Daver stepped onto the first rung of the ladder and collapsed, whimpering. "It hurts, Evren. They...they beat me bad."

"I know." Evren helped his friend stand. "But you have to be strong now, Daver."

"You're the strong one, Evren," Daver said in a weak whisper. "You always were."

"And now it's your turn." Evren gripped Daver's shoulder. "We have to go before we're discovered. But if you don't think you can do it, then I'm staying. I won't leave without you."

"I bloody will!" Rosser snapped, then hauled himself up the ladder without waiting.

"Come on, Daver," Evren persisted. "You've got to do this. It's the only way we'll be free."

"Free." Daver spoke the word in a dreamy voice. "We'll be free."

The smaller apprentice gritted his teeth and stepped onto the rope ladder. He whimpered as his tunic pulled tight over the wounds on his back, yet he didn't stop climbing. Evren's heart clenched as Daver swayed halfway up the ladder, but after a moment of rest, the boy continued. It seemed an eternity before Daver reached the top and swung up onto the wall.

Hauling himself up the rope ladder, Evren clambered onto the wall and peered into the alley below. To his relief, he found Tomaz helping Daver to the ground. Swain stood a short distance away, pawing through their now-full sacks. Gold, silver, brass, and bronze glinted in the moonlight, and the sacks sagged with the weight of their burden. Evren caught Swain's covert movements as the Claws' leader shoved a small white-gold statuette into his pocket.

Evren gathered up the ladder and dropped it in a bundle onto the muddy alley, then slithered down the remaining rope ladder. He rushed over to Daver, who leaned against the stone wall, panting with the exertion.

"You did it!" Evren clasped Daver's hand.

"I just…kept thinking…of what you'd do," Daver gasped. "I was…strong like you."

"Tomaz." Swain's voice echoed from behind Evren. "Get this loot out of here and back to the Warren."

"What about you?" Tomaz asked.

"I'll hide out nearby with Rosser and the newbies, keep an ear out for any sign of pursuit. I know a good place to lay low until morning." Swain spoke quickly. "The moment you get back to the Warren, get the boys out on the street. If the Wardens start hunting us, I want to know."

"You sure?" Tomaz asked. "This close to the temple, this turf belongs to—"

"Of course I'm sure," Swain snapped. "Don't question my orders!"

"Got it, boss." Tomaz shot a glance at Evren before turning to gather up the sacks of stolen goods. "Good luck! See you in the morning."

Evren's senses immediately went on full alert as he watched the boy disappear down the alley. Swain's plan *could* be a smart one—staying out of sight would be the best choice after what he'd done to Lectern Uman—but something about it felt wrong.

"Need a hand with him?" Swain asked. His tone was just on the wrong side of polite—the leader of the Claws didn't do polite. "I can have Rosser help you—"

"I've got him." Evren passed the bundled tunic and hidden knife to his right hand, then used his left to drape Daver's arm over his shoulder and lift the boy to his feet. "You said you know of a good hiding spot?"

"Yeah." Swain nodded. "This way."

Evren's body went cold—not the numb detachment he got when facing Lectern Uman, but the icy calm before a fight. He kept his expression nonchalant, but he tracked Swain and Rosser's every movement as they led the way down the alley.

Swain and Rosser navigated the narrow back lanes leading away from the temples and the Court of Judgement. The buildings grew progressively more decrepit as they pushed deeper into the slums that visitors to Vothmot never saw. Here, the constructions were made with rotting wood and crumbling bricks rather than sturdy stone.

The Claws' leader turned down a debris-clogged lane and motioned toward one of the few solid-looking buildings in the neighborhood.

"In here," he whispered. "We'll be safe until morning."

The door of the single-story house was unlocked, and Rosser led the way into the darkened interior. Moonlight shone through holes in the thatched straw roof, revealing rotted wooden floors, walls of bricks older than the Empty Mountains, and sagging support pillars. The house had a rear door, barred by a heavy beam—one of the few bits of wood that hadn't yet succumbed to age and termites. A barrel blocked what looked like a boarded-up pet entrance, the sort Lectern Ordari had installed on his door to allow his hound to come and go at will.

As Evren helped Daver sit against the rear wall, a loud *thunk* echoed in the house behind him. Ice ran down his spine.

"You know what, perhaps I misspoke," Swain said behind him. His voice had lost its hushed urgency and now echoed with a cold, cruel finality. "It's not *we* who will be safe in here. If the Lecterns come, Rosser and I will be nowhere in sight."

Evren turned and found Rosser standing before the now-barred front door, his arms folded over his chest. Swain had drawn his long hunting knife, and a cruel smile twisted his face.

"As for you," the Claws' leader said, "you and your brother will be dead."

Chapter Eleven

Evren's mind raced, but his face was calm as he stared at Swain. "Why?" He'd expected the Claws' leader to double-cross him, but it made more sense to do it while he was still inside the temple. He didn't understand the reasoning behind the betrayal now that they were free and clear. In fact, it didn't make much sense at all. He'd proven his value by beating Swain's rival that morning. A clever leader wouldn't waste a resource like that without good cause.

"Because of who you are." Swain shrugged. "The Lecterns aren't the sort to let their apprentices run away. They won't stop hunting until they find you. Or your bodies."

Evren's heart sank. "And let me guess, the heist gives you the perfect excuse for you to kill us. You drop that trinket you pocketed next to our corpses, and suddenly the theft is pinned on us."

"I see all those blows to your head haven't turned you into a total idiot." Swain grinned. "It's almost a shame you're more useful to me dead than alive. Now all I have to do is go to the Wardens tomorrow as a concerned citizen and report the murder I witnessed. When the Wardens find your bodies here, on the Pincers' turf, it won't take much thought for them to put two and two together."

Of course. Evren's heart sank. "They'll capture and execute the Pincers, meaning *you* can take over their turf."

"Soon, the Claws will be the most powerful street gang in Vothmot, with me as their head," Swain crowed. "We'll be stronger than the Crooked Hand ever was, and in a year's time, we'll have control of the entire city. Any gangs that don't join us will be crushed."

"A clever plan," Evren admitted. "I see just one tiny flaw. We're not dead yet."

Swain snorted. "Easily remedied." He turned to Rosser. "Kill him."

Doubt flashed in Rosser's eyes, but only for a moment. He moved away from the door and stepped toward Evren.

Evren squared off, fists raised, the same stance he'd used to take Hakim and Engerack down. "You sure you want to do this?" he asked, his face going hard. "Remember Engerack."

Rosser hesitated mid-step, then stopped. He turned to Swain. "Boss, maybe we're better off—"

"Do it!" Swain shouted. His face purpled with rage, and a wild light shone in his eyes. "I am your boss! Obey my orders."

"But, boss—"

Swain stepped up to Rosser and, with the speed of a darting snake, slashed the boy's throat. Rosser gasped and clapped his hands to the gushing wound.

"I have no use for cowards in my ranks," Swain snarled and drove the dagger into the boy's chest. Blood splashed his clothing, face, and hands as he pulled the blade free. Rosser's collapsing body hit the wooden floor of the building with a loud *thump*. He lay still, wide eyes fixed on Evren, horror written in his gaze.

Evren was too stunned by Swain's cruelty to take advantage of his momentary distraction. By the time he blinked away his surprise, the Claw leader had turned a bloodstained glare on Evren. "Your turn," he sneered.

Evren's eyes never left the Claws' leader as he wrapped his tunic around his right hand. Only a fool went into a knife-fight bare-handed.

Swain rolled his eyes. "A broken knife? Pathetic!"

Evren ignored the taunt. He'd never wielded a dagger, but he'd watched enough knife-fights among the apprentices to know they always ended with both combatants bleeding.

Swain, however, seemed perfectly comfortable with his blade. He moved in a low crouch, weight resting on the balls of his feet. His knife never stopped weaving circles in the air. Evren tensed, and it took effort to wrest his eyes from the blade. Watching the weapon was a mistake; he had to keep his eyes on Swain's body, to anticipate the boy's movements and attacks.

He saw the quick forward shuffle coming and was already ducking the blow when Swain slashed high with his knife. But he wasn't fast enough to evade the blade completely. He sucked in a breath as the dagger carved a line of fire into his left shoulder, then continued traveling upward to gouge his scalp just above the ear.

Swain whipped the blade across in a backhand stroke, and Evren threw himself backward just in time to evade the slashing blow that would have carved open his forehead. Swain came on fast and low, his knife stabbing a dozen times in the space of two seconds. Evren gave ground but circled to his left instead of retreating backward. He had to stay on Swain's weaker side, force the boy to use less-controlled backhand attacks.

"Clever, clever, clever," Swain growled, a wicked smile twisting his lips. "Thinking you can avoid my dominant hand. How about this?" He tossed the knife to his left hand, then came at Evren in a rush.

This time, Evren didn't dodge the slashing strike aimed at his neck but stepped forward and raised his left arm in a cross-block that caught Swain's forearm. At the same time, he dropped his right arm and brought the stump of the dagger thrusting toward Swain's armpit. Swain spun out of the way at the last moment, but the severed blade caught him along the ribs.

Swain bellowed and charged, his knife driving at Evren's chest, stomach, neck, face, and legs. Only instinct and years spent dodging powerful punches saved Evren from being stabbed. He twisted and slipped out of the way, then brought his own dagger up toward Swain's chin. When the Claw ducked to the side to evade the blow, Evren drove his left fist into the boy's face.

The force of the punch rocked Swain back on his heels, and Evren followed up with two more quick jabs. The moment Swain's knife hand dropped, Evren slashed his blade along the boy's forearm. Swain hissed again and his knife clattered to the ground.

But he recovered quickly and rushed Evren, arms outstretched. It was the same move Engerack had used on him in his cell, but Swain was far smaller than the seventh-year apprentice. Evren stepped back with his right foot, shifted his weight to his left, then drove his knee up into Swain's face. Bone and cartilage *crunched*, and the force of the blow knocked Swain to the side. He collapsed to the floor, his face striking hard wood with jarring impact. Evren leapt atop Swain's back before the boy could recover and drove his knee into the spinal column—not hard enough to shatter bone but enough to send a clear message.

"Enough, Swain!" Evren cried. He pressed the stump of his knife blade against the side of the boy's neck. "I don't want to have to hurt you."

"Coward!" Swain snarled through broken teeth and split lips. "You're too weak to kill me, just like Rosser and Tomaz and all the rest of them. You're all weaklings, which is why none of you will ever be a leader. You don't have what it takes to—"

Evren slammed the pommel of his kitchen knife into the base of Swain's skull, and the flow of vitriol fell quiet. Silence filled the small building. Evren drew in a deep breath, then winced at the ache in his ribs. The dagger wound in his shoulder stung, which only added to the pain in his face, head, chest, and stomach. He'd taken too many beatings tonight.

His mind raced as he tried to figure out his next move. If he killed Swain, he and Daver could return to the Claws. The street gang might believe a tale about Rosser and Swain being caught by the Wardens, and there would be no one to dispute his story. Perhaps he could even lead the Claws, using his skill with his fists to protect them from the other gangs.

Yet, just as with Lectern Uman, he couldn't bring himself to kill. Swain was his enemy, and he wouldn't stop until Evren and Daver were dead. But he'd be no better than Swain if he murdered the unconscious boy. Swain might be a cruel, vicious, bloodthirsty bastard, but Evren wasn't. He wouldn't let Swain's decisions define his.

A wild idea came to his mind. Before he could reconsider, he unwrapped the tunic from his right hand and used the edge of his shattered knife to cut it into long strips. He bound Swain's ankles, knees, and wrists, then stuffed a wad of cloth into the boy's mouth for good measure.

He sat back on his heels, staring down at the unconscious Claw. What now? He couldn't report the boy to the Wardens—he needed to stay as far away from the city guards as possible, especially after tonight's robbery and Lectern Uman's death. Maybe if he brought Swain back to the Claws and explained what had happened, they would deal with him their way. He had no idea what sort of justice or punishment they'd inflict, but at least *he* wouldn't be the one to kill Swain.

"Oh, Swaaaaain!" The singsong voice from outside the building snapped Evren from his thoughts. "Swaaainy Swaaain!"

Heart hammering, Evren crept over to the window and peered out.

Ten figures stood arrayed in front of the building holding torches and oil lanterns. Evren immediately recognized the one at the front: taller than the rest of his crew, with oddly rich clothing, a handsome face, and a scar over his right eyebrow.

"Come out, Swain!" shouted Hakim, leader of the Pincers. "We've a score to settle tonight."

Chapter Twelve

Evren ducked below the window before the Pincers caught sight of him and walked in a low crouch back to where Daver still sat against the wall.

"We're in trouble, Daver," he said in a low voice. "Those guys outside are here for Swain, but they'll be pissed at me, too. We've got to hope they don't have anyone watching the back way out. Once we're outside, we're going to have to run. Think you can make it?"

"I-I'll try," Daver replied, his voice weak.

Evren turned to the house's back door and struggled to lift the heavy locking bar holding it closed. With effort, he managed to get one end of the beam off its supports, then dropped it to the ground and hauled at the other end.

"Not coming out, Swain?" Hakim called from out front. "I know you're in there. The Mistress smiled on us tonight, she did. Just our luck to find you here on our turf, with just a few of your gang to keep you company."

Evren shoved hard on the door, but it only opened a hand's breadth before *clunking* against something solid. He tried again, and again the door refused to budge.

"Damn it!" He shoved his face into the crack in an attempt to see what was blocking the way. He caught the barest glimpse of debris piled high in the alleyway outside the door.

"There's no way out, Swaaaaaiin!" Hakim sang out. "That back alley's piled so high with crap there's no way you're getting out and, if you try anything, I've got two of my boys ready to bring you down. Your only choice is to come out the front door and take your beating like a man. I promise I'll stop my lads before they break every bone in your body."

Evren's gut clenched as he pushed. True to Hakim's words, the debris was piled high outside the door. No way he'd get the door open from inside.

He whirled and scanned the rest of the room for any other way out. The single-story house had no windows, and the crumbling roof wouldn't support Daver's weight, much less his. Ten boys waited for him outside the front door. The moment Hakim saw his face, he'd order his crew to fight. Evren could take a few, but not that many.

"Last chaaaance!" Hakim called. "Come out like a man or die like a coward."

Evren's mind raced. What could he do? He was trapped. If he was alone, he'd risk breaking out the front and fighting his way through the boys. But with Daver in tow, he couldn't take the chance. Daver was already too weak from one beating; he wouldn't survive another.

"You made a mistake coming here," Hakim said. His voice had lost the mocking singsong tone, replaced by a hard edge. "What sort of leader would I be if I let your actions from this morning stand?"

Dread writhed in Evren's gut, but he clenched his fists. Crouching, he slithered through the darkness toward the front door. If he opened the door, maybe he could lure Hakim's crew into the house. He'd be outnumbered, but he might be able to surprise the Pincers long enough to make an opening for Daver to escape.

A *crash* echoed from the outside of the house, and something wet and viscous splashed through the cracks in the door. The acrid odor of lamp oil reached Evren's nostrils, accompanied by half a dozen more *crashes*. A clay jar flew through the window and shattered on the floor beside Rosser, spraying oil across the dead Claw.

"Don't say I didn't warn you!"

A torch hurtled into the room and landed a finger's breadth from the puddle of oil. Evren had a second to dive back toward Daver before the fuel ignited. A loud *whoosh* filled the little house and flames licked across the wooden floor. Within seconds, the bright tongues of fire engulfed Rosser's body.

Evren stared in horror as an oil lamp sailed through the window and landed a hand's breadth from the bound and gagged Swain. Liquid flame splashed across the ground, and one tongue of fire latched onto Swain's pant leg.

Without hesitation, Evren leapt across the room, caught Swain by the shirt, and dragged him away from the window. He beat at the flames eating through the unconscious boy's pants until only charred cloth remained.

But another jar of oil flew through the window, followed by a torch that lit it on fire. By the time Evren wrestled Swain's body away from the flames, the entire house was a blazing inferno.

The light of the burning roof and walls illuminated the interior of the building, and Evren's heart leapt as he caught sight of the boarded-up pet entrance. He threw his shoulder against the barrel and strained to roll it aside, then set about wrestling with the wooden boards covering the opening.

His heart sank as he ripped the last board free. His shoulders would never fit through there.

"Let me," Daver said.

Evren whirled to find the smaller boy standing beside him.

Daver bent to study the compact entrance. "I can fit."

"Go!" Evren moved aside. "I just need you to clear me a path so I can open the back door and drag Swain out."

"You'd save him?" Daver asked, wide-eyed. "After what he tried to do?"

"He might be a bastard," Evren said, "but we don't have to be." The Lecterns' abuse hadn't broken him; he wouldn't let Swain's viciousness define who he was.

Daver got to his hands and knees and shoved his head through the small gap. A few moments of scrabbling at the debris outside got him through, and Evren's heart leapt as Daver's feet disappeared. He stooped, seized Swain's tunic, and hauled the unconscious Claw toward the rear door.

The crackling of the fire grew louder, and the beams of the roof began to collapse at the front of the house. Entire sections of the northern and western wall crumbled from the heat of the flames. In less than a minute, the entire house would come down around him.

Evren tightened his grip on Swain's collar and kept dragging the unconscious boy the last few paces to the door. The fabric of Swain's shirt ripped, and Evren fell backward, a shred of torn cloth in his hand. He quickly recovered and reached for Swain again. His hands had just closed around Swain's shirt when a roof beam collapsed right in front of him.

Swain gave a weak "uggh" as the heavy wooden support slammed into his chest, crushing his ribs and midsection. Blood spattered Evren's face, and Swain's eyes flew wide. His lips moved but no sound came out. With a weak gasp, Swain's eyes rolled back and his head sagged to one side.

Evren felt that same cold chill seeping into his body as he stared at the dead Claw. For a moment, the heat of the burning roof beam was forgotten in the horror of watching Swain die right in front of him.

"Evren!" The back door muffled Daver's voice. "Evren, I think I've cleared enough for you to get out."

The words snapped Evren from his trance. He turned to go, when glinting metal caught his eye. Around Swain's neck hung the Lectern's pendant he'd taken from Evren two days earlier.

Swain's words from earlier popped into Evren's head. "The Lecterns aren't the sort to let their apprentices run away. They won't stop hunting until they find you. Or your bodies."

Swain had been right. The Lecterns would only give up the hunt if they believed Daver and Evren were dead.

Swain was the same size as Evren, and he wore Evren's crescent moon pendant. Once the fire had burned away his features, no one would be able to tell Swain's corpse apart from his.

He whirled toward the back door. "Daver!" He threw his shoulder against the wood with every ounce of strength. The door scraped against crumbled bricks and piled debris but slid open enough for him to see the smaller apprentice outside. "Daver, give me your pendant, now!"

"Why?"

"Just do it!" Evren insisted.

Firelight gleamed on the crescent moon pendant Daver held out. Evren snatched it up, turned, and dropped the necklace into Swain's outstretched hand. The platinum would survive the fire. If the Mistress' luck smiled on him, the Wardens and Lecterns would believe Evren had died trying to escape the fire. The two pendants would tie the two corpses to the missing apprentices. It was the best he could hope for.

He turned and ran, and with two running steps crashed into the back door. The hinges groaned and the wood bent, but the door swung wide enough for him to squeeze through. He tripped over the debris piled high and landed face-first in a pile of muck.

"Let's go!" He scrambled to his feet and clambered onto the piles of crumbled brick and human detritus. "We've got to get far away from here before the Wardens come to investigate the fire."

He slogged through the ankle-deep muck—a foul mixture of stagnant rainwater, urine, and the Keeper knew what else. The stink assaulted his nostrils, but the smoke of the burning building grew thicker with every passing second.

Evren tensed in expectation of a fight as he approached the mouth of the alleyway. Hakim had said he had people watching the alleyway. His heart sank as he caught sight of the young boy standing against the wall at the far end of the narrow lane. He clung to the shadows, grateful for the crackling of the fire to conceal the sound of his movements through the debris. The lookout's attention was so fixated on the pillar of fire consuming the house that he failed to notice Evren slipping through the darkness. Evren dropped the night-blind boy with a single punch to the jaw.

He cast a glance toward the main avenue in time to see mirror-armored Wardens running toward the blaze, white cloaks streaming behind them. Seizing Daver's hand, he raced deeper into the back alleys and away from the temple.

Toward freedom.

Epilogue

Evren pulled his stolen hat lower and bent forward to hide his face. He glanced back at Daver, who stumbled alongside him. The smaller boy looked exhausted—a night spent running and hiding among the back-alleys around the Court of Judgement hadn't done his battered body much good—but he tried his best to keep pace. Evren knew the rough-spun clothing they'd stolen would rub the wounds on Daver's back raw, yet Daver hadn't voiced complaint. They both knew the importance of finding a way to safety.

Evren had only one place he could consider safe right now.

His legs wobbled as he teetered the last few steps toward the Summer Market and Kaltris' still-closed stall, and a sigh of relief escaped his lips.

Jodech glanced up at his approach, and the man's dark eyes went wide. "Keeper's beard, lad, what happened to you?" Concern furrowing his sun-darkened forehead.

"Someone thought we had something worth stealing," Evren replied as he helped Daver to a seat against a nearby wall. His answer wasn't a complete lie—the white-gold statuette in his pocket would make any mugger's day.

"Bright Lady have mercy!" Cheeril shook her head, which set her red braids flying. "And to think I came to this city to get *away* from all the crime in Praamis. It's like the Night Guild all over again!"

"You talking about last night's fire?" Jodech asked.

Evren's ears perked up. Gossip traveled fast in marketplaces. The information would be distorted in the retelling, but it might contain a few scraps of truth.

"Aye," Cheeril said with a nod. "Neighbor of mine was near the Court of Judgement when it happened. Saw the whole thing, he did. Said a gang of street toughs set fire to a buildin'." She leaned closer to Jodech and dropped her voice to a whisper. "Killed two apprentice Lecterns, I hear. The Master's priests are spittin' hellfire and ready to send every Warden in the city into the district to root out the criminals."

"Two apprentices, eh?" Jodech toyed with his long, dark braid. "Might be the two who ran away from the temple, then?"

Cheeril shrugged. "I don't know nothin' about that. All's I know's what my neighbor told me."

Evren's heart leapt as he listened to the two continue their gossip. If the Wardens believed the corpses belonged to him and Daver, they had a chance at starting a brand new life.

Hope surged within him as he spotted a familiar mule-drawn wagon rumbling up the road toward the market.

Kaltris' face brightened at the sight of Evren and Daver. "Good to see you, lads!" he called out as he drew his wagon to a halt behind his stall. "Had you on my mind the whole way to Brittlewall and back."

The old merchant clambered down from his wagon with a groan and a loud *clicking* of his joints. When he finally dismounted, he turned to Evren. "You give my offer any thought?"

"I have," Evren said. "And I've got another offer for you."

"That so?" One white eyebrow climbed toward Kaltris' bald scalp. "What's that?"

"You take my brother." Evren motioned to Daver, who had leaned his head against the wall and closed his eyes.

"I already told you I can only take one of you. You're the one—"

"He's the one who needs to be taken care of," Evren insisted. "I can look after myself, but Daver, he's…" He swallowed. "He's not cut out for a life on the streets."

"I need a strong lad." Kaltris held up his hands. "I can do the sums well enough, but what I can't do is load and unload my wagon."

"Then, I'll do it for you." Evren wouldn't give up. "You don't even have to pay me. I'll come and do your heavy lifting until Daver's strong enough to do it."

Kaltris' eyes narrowed, and his expression grew pensive.

"Please," Evren begged. "I need him to be safe. You're his only hope of a better life, a life away from the streets. I'll do whatever it takes to make that happen."

After a moment, Kaltris nodded. "I'll take him in, lad. And don't worry about doing my heavy lifting. There are plenty of young men I can hire until Daver's able to take over."

Relief flooded Evren, and he felt as if a massive burden had been lifted from his shoulders. "Thank you, Kaltris," he said, his throat thick. "Thank you."

"It's nothing." Kaltris gave a dismissive wave. Though his tone was gruff, a hint of moisture sparkled in his eyes. "It'll be good having someone around to help out. But you better come around and visit, you hear? Might be I can spare the occasional bit of produce now and again."

Evren nodded. "I will."

"What are you going to do?" Kaltris asked in a quiet voice.

Evren drew in a deep breath. "I…don't know." His eyes strayed toward the Master's Temple rising in the distance. It was a beautiful white marble structure that stood twice the height of the city wall, with a blue glass dome for a crown and seven minarets standing guard around it. Even now, the voices of the Lecterns atop the towers rang out across Vothmot as they called out the morning prayer. "For years, I've had people telling me what to do, what my future'll hold. But now there's none of that. In a way, that feels…"

Kaltris smiled. "Liberating?"

"Sure." Evren nodded. "It's a good thing, knowing I can choose to do whatever I want with my life."

"Make good choices, lad." Kaltris placed a gnarled hand on his shoulder. "Your future might not always be clear, but if you focus on doing right in the present, things have a way of sorting themselves out." He gave Evren a wry smile. "Who knows, one day we might read about the great hero Evren in the history books."

Evren snorted. "Not likely! You don't even know how to read."

"Fair enough." Kaltris grinned. "Apprentice be with you, lad."

"And you, Master Kaltris."

A lump rose in Evren's throat as he turned to Daver. Tears glimmered in the smaller boy's eyes. "Are you really leaving me, Evren?"

"It's for the best, Daver." Evren wrestled against tears of his own. "Kaltris will give you a home, a trade, a future."

"But without you!" Daver clutched at Evren's arms, his gaze sorrowful.

Evren gripped the boy's hand. "No, I'll be around. Someone's got to keep an eye on you, make sure you stay out of trouble." He swallowed hard. "Besides, if you're going to be running a business, we can't have all the gangs in Vothmot swiping your fruit. I'll keep them in line, I promise."

Daver wiped his eyes. "Promise you'll visit every day."

"I swear it." Evren placed a hand over his heart. "On all the gods of Einan. If I break this oath, may my soul suffer in the darkest hells for all eternity." He ruffled the smaller boy's hair. "Good enough?"

Daver nodded and scrubbed away the last of his tears. "Yes."

Evren stood, and a smile broke out on his lips. "See you tomorrow, Daver?"

"I'll be here."

Evren turned and, with a farewell wave to Kaltris, Jodech, and Cheeril, strode up the street toward the Prime Bazaar.

For the first time in his life, he had nothing he *had* to do, no duties, chores, or lessons to dread. He was his own man, able to make his own choices. If he wanted, he could join up with the Pincers, take control of the Claws, or run on his own. Hell, he could do whatever he wanted.

His smile widened as he pushed through the press of people flooding Vothmot's crowded marketplace. He was free of his past, and the future was his to choose. He couldn't wait to find out what sort of adventures lay ahead.

Author's Note

The Renegade Apprentice is a prequel novella introducing Evren, a character that is critical to TWO other series:

- He's a supporting character in **Darkblade Slayer (Hero of Darkness Book 5),** where the knowledge he has gained over years working in the Master's Temple proves crucial to the Hunter's search for the Lost City of Enarium.

- He is one of the primary characters in the **Heirs of Destiny** series, which follows his adventures in Shalandra, the City of the Dead (along with characters from both the **Hero of Darkness** and **Queen of Thieves** series)

Evren is the very definition of defiance, courage, and internal fortitude despite everything he's had to endure at the hands of the Lecterns. He is a character that I LOVED writing from the moment he first slipped his way onto the pages of Darkblade Slayer and did the one thing no one in their right mind would dare to do: he stole the Hunter of Voramis' purse.

I hope you'll join me for the rest of Evren's journey in both series!

More Books by Andy Peloquin

Queen of Thieves
Book 1: Child of the Night Guild
Book 2: Thief of the Night Guild
Book 3: Queen of the Night Guild

Traitors' Fate (**Queen of Thieves/Hero of Darkness Crossover**)

Hero of Darkness
Book 1: Darkblade Assassin
Book 2: Darkblade Outcast
Book 3: Darkblade Protector
Book 4: Darkblade Seeker
Book 5: Darkblade Slayer
Book 6: Darkblade Savior
Book 7: Darkblade Justice

Heirs of Destiny
Book 1: Trial of Stone
Book 2: Crucible of Fortune
Book 3: Storm of Chaos
Book 4: Secrets of Blood
Book 5: Ascension of Death
Book 6: The Renegade Apprentice

Different, Not Damaged: A Short Story Collection

About the Author

I am, first and foremost, a storyteller and an artist--words are my palette. Fantasy is my genre of choice, and I love to explore the darker side of human nature through the filter of fantasy heroes, villains, and everything in between. I'm also a freelance writer, a book lover, and a guy who just loves to meet new people and spend hours talking about my fascination for the worlds I encounter in the pages of fantasy novels.

Fantasy provides us with an escape, a way to forget about our mundane problems and step into worlds where anything is possible. It transcends age, gender, religion, race, or lifestyle--it is our way of believing what cannot be, delving into the unknowable, and discovering hidden truths about ourselves and our world in a brand new way. Fiction at its very best!

Join my Facebook Reader Group
for updates, LIVE readings, exclusive content, and all-around fantasy fun.
Let's Get Social!
Be My Friend: https://www.facebook.com/andrew.peloquin.1
Facebook Author Page: https://www.facebook.com/andyqpeloquin
Twitter: https://twitter.com/AndyPeloquin

Made in the USA
Columbia, SC
07 June 2023

17810736R00064